BECAUSE
YOU WERE
THERE

JOAN LEWIS

CRANTHORPE
—MILLNER—
PUBLISHERS

First published by Cranthorpe Millner Publishers (2023)

ISBN 978-1-80378-112-9 (Paperback)

www.cranthorpemillner.com

Cranthorpe Millner Publishers

'I'm not a monkey, I'm a human being.
How you want me to feel about England?
It hurts here.
It really hurts.'

Paulette Wilson
1956 – 2020
Windrush victim

Tina
Roytown, Jamaica
May 13th 1968

> *'Dis poetry stays wid me when I run or walk*
> *An when I am talking to meself in poetry I talk,*
> *Dis poetry is wid me*
> *Below me an above,*
> *Dis poetry's from inside me*
> *It goes to yu*
> *WID LUV.'*

from *Dis Poetry*, by Benjamin Zephaniah

"Hush yuh mout everybady. Mi cyaan tink." Tina put her hands over her ears and ran ahead.

What with all those birds squawking from the banana palms, and everyone shouting at her, she was feeling quite dizzy. Janine caught her up and hung her arm around her friend's shoulder. They stepped up their pace leaving the others in their wake. Tina's rucksack was heavier than usual. She had been told to clear her desk, and it was bumping now against the small of her back as she ran. She was going to miss school. Mr Williams had said it was a great pity that she wouldn't be going on to the new secondary school after grade six, because she was his star pupil. He had told her nana that too.

As the girls reached the big school, more kids were pouring out to join them in an endless stream of blue and khaki uniforms that jostled and joked their way home. Even the older kids seemed to know that she was leaving for England tomorrow and they shouted out their best wishes to her. She felt a bit like a celebrity. No-one around there had ever been on a plane before.

First they passed the Anglican Church, then the food store and the bank, the Baptist Church, and last of all the church that Tina attended every Sunday, the Church of the Adventists. This stood on the very edge of town. One by one the school kids had fallen away, as the number of dwellings thinned out, and the tarmac road turned to beaten red earth. Tina and Janine had the furthest to go. Their neighbouring homesteads were nearly an hour's walk from the town, but they were such best friends that they agreed this was one of the nicest parts of the day.

A battered old car approached them from behind, weaving its way carefully between the chatting girls and a giant pothole. It stopped briefly just ahead of them. Tina's Uncle James wound down his window further to greet the girls, while conveniently allowing a few stray goats to straggle safely past. Then, as he coaxed the car back into life, he resumed his climb, waving his enormous hand through the open window in farewell. There had been no room in the car for the girls today as it was so jam-packed with stuff. Tina prayed that it would be cleared in time for her journey to the airport in Montego Bay the following morning.

Janine's house came first, with its shocking pink fence and tidy lime-green painted veranda, which always made Tina smile. It was a long time since her nana's house had looked so cheerful, for its walls and paintwork were peeling nowadays. But then it did feel like home, and the garden, with its brilliant pink bougainvillea flowers, breadfruit and yellow mangoes made up for it all.

Janine was crying now as they gave each other a hug of farewell, but Tina felt confident that she'd be back before too long, so she didn't feel too sad.

"Mi wi si yuh soon," she said, comforting her.

When Tina reached home, she saw that her uncle was busy in the yard unloading armfuls of yam sticks through the car window, while struggling to kick aside a chicken that was getting under his feet.

The next morning the car was clear, ready and waiting for its honoured guest. Tina was wearing her best cotton frock, knee length white socks and a new hat. Her case had been packed with all her clothes and placed on the back seat while, for the first time in her life, she was to sit in the front. People were hugging her now and kissing her smack on the lips. Cousins, aunts, uncles, everyone was crowding around her and wishing her well. It was bedlam. Her nana was the last one to approach. She held her long and tight, squashing her

3

nose hard against her cushiony bosom. Then she pushed her away in order to gaze at Tina's scrubbed face and those tight braids that were escaping from underneath her straw hat. It felt as if her nana was hoping to store that image for ever.

Tina was in a whirl. She felt enormously excited to think that she would soon be with her mum, living and going to school in a town called Dunborough. She'd never been away from Jamaica before in her whole life. Last night she had dreamed of England: a confusion of red buses; nurses in starched white aprons; princes and queens; policemen in helmets; and endless white faces peering down at her as she sweated and tossed about on her narrow bed. But all was forgotten now in the rush to catch that plane. She didn't even have time to consider that she might miss Jamaica.

Tina
Gatwick Airport, England
May 14th 1968

Tina hadn't enjoyed being on the plane. That first lurch up into the sky had been scary, and she had kept her eyes shut for a long time afterwards. Even when she opened them again, she hardly dared to look out of the little porthole, preferring to watch all the different people who were sitting around her. The nice hostess had given her snacks and a book of puzzles to do, and she kept coming over to make sure that Tina was all right. There had been a long wait on the tarmac while the plane refuelled at Bermuda. Tina dreaded going through a second take-off, but this time it hadn't felt so bad. After that she had fallen into a deep sleep as her early life slipped away, and a new one began.

Everybody clapped and cheered when the plane finally landed in England. But when Tina dared to look outside again she didn't think it looked so great. All she could see were lots of grey clouds glowering over the wet grey tarmac.

The hostess brought Tina, and a younger boy from Kingston, to the arrivals gate. After helping them collect their cases, it was her job to hand them over safely to their families. Tina had pictured her mum standing there waving and smiling in her smart nurse's uniform. But try as she might, she couldn't see her anywhere amongst that big crowd. She had never seen so many white people before. She felt devastated and lost as she fought against her tears. Everyone was jostling each other and staring at them as they came through the moving doors. At last Tina spotted a brown lady with lovely tight curly black hair like her own, in a big smart updo.

"Mum," she cried, pointing her out to the hostess and dancing around excitedly. But the lady turned away.

Suddenly someone else was grabbing her from behind and wrenching her away from the others to envelop her in a big sobbing hug. The hug lasted a long time. Her mum's tears were falling onto her cotton dress and she began to feel cold. She had to break free or she was going to suffocate.

"Baby luv, mi baby luv," was all her mother could say as she reached down to cup her face between her hands.

Tina was studying her mother more closely now. Somehow it felt all wrong. This person looked nothing like the photograph on the wall back home, and what on earth were those clothes that she had on? In place of the eagerly awaited nurse's uniform, she was wearing a strange kind of patterned dress that seemed to go straight down her body and end far too soon above her knees. Tina patted down the flounces on her cotton frock while casting covert glances around her. Everyone seemed to be wearing clothes like her mum. Some women even had baggy trousers on, like men, and Tina couldn't help wondering what their minister would have to say about that. What's more, there wasn't a straw hat in sight. She snatched hers from the top of her head and surreptitiously dropped it where it would be trampled on by the crowd.

Her mum was busy, now, signing something with the hostess. For the first time since she'd left home, Tina ached for her nana. Then her mum turned around.

"Cum pan darling gyal, bring yuh case. Mi bredren waiting tuh tek yuh tuh si yuh new home."

Clinging to her mum's hand, Tina walked with her towards a line of cars, where her mum's friend was waiting. He looked a bit like Tina's uncle, but more serious; there was no sign of laughter on his face, nor even a smile, not like Uncle James who laughed all the time and who always made you feel happy. This man kept frowning and saying private things to her mum as they drove away from the airport. She didn't like him one bit.

"Yuh hungry baby luv?" her mum asked, turning round to see how she was doing in the back of the car.

Tina just nodded. The whole thing felt bewildering, with cars rushing past them in both directions, and endless roads that took them through town after town.

And it was so cold too. She just sat there and shivered in her best cotton dress. Everything looked so grey. Grey clouds, grey houses, grey people, grey roads. And where on earth were all the trees?

At last Tina's mum announced that they had arrived in Dunborough. Her friend turned the car into a dark street where all the houses seemed to be touching one another. He parked in the very middle of the row. A flight of stone steps led up from the pavement towards a green painted door with a number twelve on it, and a big knocker in the shape of a hand. When Tina looked up, she saw row after row of windows and lots of chimney pots belching black smoke, which melted away into the gloomy clouds like smudges of charcoal. She wondered whether she would ever see the sun again. So, when her mum announced that this was where she was going to live, she felt fit to cry. Mum took her hand and led her towards the front door, while her 'friend' followed with her case. After another two flights of stairs, they reached the door of her mum's flat. Tina suspected that life was going to be full of staircases from now on.

That night they ate fish and chips for supper, but it didn't taste half as good as her nana's rice and peas. All of Tina's excitement about coming to England had leached away as she came to realise that Jamaica was a much better place to be.

There was a small primary school not far from their flat. Apparently, children would be breaking up for the summer holidays before long and come September Tina would be old enough to go to high school. She wondered what colour uniform she would wear and hoped it would be royal blue like the girls at Roytown. Her mum had taken the next day off work so that she could register her as a pupil, and after breakfast Tina found herself sitting next to her mum in the headmaster's office at Dunborough Church of England Primary School. He seemed very kind, but how she wished the grown-ups would stop talking so that she could go and see what her classroom looked like, meet some other girls, and maybe even make a special friend like Janine. But what was this man saying? She wasn't even going to go into a proper class because she was a bit 'behind' with her language. She would have to go into a smaller group for assessment instead. And now the headmaster was saying that he thought she may not even cope with secondary school. Didn't he know that she had been her teacher's star pupil? What's more, she had been looking forward to going to high school for ever and ever. There were only three others in her group. One boy called Richard from Trinidad, one little white girl who looked like a mouse and didn't say much, and a girl called Maisie who said she was from Jamaica too.

Every day when they went into the hall for school dinners, or outside for playtime, Maisie would run off and leave her alone. Nobody wanted to make friends with Tina and they often called her names, so Tina was delighted when the summer holidays were about to begin. She wasn't so sure about the idea of her mum going to work though and leaving her alone every day.

"Wah mek nuh wi guh a di seaside before yuh guh back tuh school?" her mum had suggested.

Tina had liked that idea very much and hoped fervently that her mum's friend would stay away so that she could have her mum to herself.

In the first week of the holidays, Tina's mum received a letter from the education authority.

"Yuh wi guh a a special school inna di new term," she announced. "Mi goodness yuh lucky. Mi a guh write tuh yuh nana. It wi mek har suh proud."

*

When September arrived, Tina was left in no doubt whatsoever that her treatment was indeed very 'special'. On the first day of term, as other kids in the street were walking to school in their new uniforms, a large black car pulled up outside Tina's door. It was a taxi, and it was going to take her all the way to her new school on the edge of town.

Sitting alongside her on the back seat were two other kids who kept staring at her as if she had just landed from the moon. Plonking herself back against the seat, she pulled a face and then stuck her tongue out at them. They weren't worth bothering with. Tina soon discovered, however, that most of the children at the school were harmless enough. In fact, they seemed fairly dumb, apart from a couple of girls with whom she quickly teamed up, and who taught her how to give 'backchat' to the teachers. The teachers were quite nice too, on the whole, fairly easy going, although they didn't seem to expect very much of her. But Mr Evans, their form teacher, was different. She'd never seen a white man with red hair before. He was tall and heavy and would snarl at you for no reason whatsoever if you came too close, like a caged lion. She already disliked him intensely. But Tina knew she could cope, even when he made comments about her that she didn't like. It was some of those timid boys that she felt most sorry for. He would shout at them and threaten to hit them with a book or a ruler, even though they were far too soft to do anything wrong. He liked to creep up close, then shout so loud and sudden that it made you jump out of your skin. How she missed Mr Williams. How she longed for his kind and gentle ways and that soft, sing-song voice which made poetry as he spoke.

By the beginning of the second week, Tina had begun to loathe school. She had dreamed of going to high school and wearing a uniform like all the other kids for such a long time. But this was completely different. The school didn't even have its own uniform, and she certainly didn't like wearing these strange new clothes her mum had bought for her. She wanted a long royal blue pinafore dress and white shirt like Janine would be wearing back home. The only things that made going to school bearable were those delicious school dinners and the kind teacher who taught them to cook and sew. Tina used to be good at maths and she loved writing stories. But nobody seemed to ask her to do those sorts of things anymore. When she got bored and looked around for some interesting books to read, she found that the shelves were almost bare.

"Everything dem mek mi duh far too easy peasy," she had complained to her mum when she got home.

As she stood outside her front door one chilly Monday morning in September, ready to jump down the stone steps and into the taxi, she conjured up a plan. When the taxi driver called up for her to come as usual and held the car door open for her, she would run right past him. She definitely wouldn't look up. She would just keep on running and running with her head down. At the end of their street, she would stop. Then, refusing to look back, she would turn into the busy main road and carefully follow the pavement all the way; past the shops and cafés; past the pubs and fancy hotels; past all the people and gawking tourists; past the church and past the river that runs under the bridge. She would keep on running and running until finally she had left all the houses behind. And still she would run and run until she could hardly grab a breath and her sides hurt. But she wouldn't care, because now she would notice that all the dirty cars and lorries had vanished, and that the road was turning to dry beaten earth. Then the warm moist wind would sing to her and stir up the fat banana palm leaves above her head. And still she would run and run and run until finally, there in the distance, she would spot Janine's homestead, all pink and green, and her one true friend standing on the pretty veranda waving and jumping about like a wild thing. But best of all would be the sight of her nana's house at the very top of the hill. With one last gasp of air and one final burst, she would be there. Uncle James would see her first and run to meet her. He would lift her up so high towards the sun with his big brown hands that she could reach out and pick a ripe mango for tea. And she would never ever go back to that hateful school again.

Felicity
Silver Moon Resort, Arthurstown, Jamaica
February 21st 2000

For some strange reason Felicity fully expected to feel at home in Jamaica, even though she had never been there before in her life. After all, she was British, and Jamaicans had very much become a part of British life. As a teacher she had got to know many Jamaican children, both in Dunborough and in London, and some of their parents too. She now harboured a feeling of sentimental affection for them and their mother country and fully expected that that bond would be reciprocated. She and Alistair had been invited to Jamaica in order to participate in a family reunion to celebrate the ruby wedding anniversary of Alistair's parents. Most of Alistair's family lived in the States, so Jamaica had been a convenient location. Her in-laws had decided that everyone should stay in a large international style resort where they were to occupy three adjacent houses overlooking the manicured silver sands. But Felicity felt disappointed by the welcome she'd received at their luxury accommodation. Her British accent had failed to provoke any reaction from the Jamaican staff whatsoever. Indeed, the strong American drawl of her husband and his family seemed to command greater interest and respect. Each lodging had a resident cook and waiting staff. Felicity noticed a chamber maid, dressed in a frilly apron and mop cap, going up and down the wide double staircase, clutching bundles of fresh linen to her chest. The racial divide between themselves and the staff unnerved her, and the faux colonial style mansion that they were to live in evoked images of *Gone with the Wind*.

"Come on, Flic. We're here to enjoy ourselves," Alistair had complained when she pointed out her misgivings. "Stop being so bloody political. Let's just make the best of this for my parents' sake."

And Felicity had. The days passed in a whirl of celebratory dinners, buggy drives, swimming and endless clinking of champagne glasses. But Felicity couldn't help feeling slightly trapped. She liked to escape the family frenzy from time to time and would often sit on their bedroom balcony with a book, looking out at the Caribbean Sea. But it was hard to ignore the captive hotel dolphin that swam in front of her, backwards and forwards within the narrow confines of a series of plastic buoys. How she longed to cut through that cruel netting and set it free, so that together they could head off towards those distant coral reefs and azure seas.

As the holiday drew to a close, it was decided that the whole family should gather in a restaurant for a final dinner. They were welcomed that night by a charming young Jamaican lady who took them to be seated in the palatial dining room of this grand house. The top-class restaurant was a short drive from the rest of the resort, but Felicity quickly realised that it was a sham. It was all part of the same international enterprise, just as the mock outlets in the shopping 'village' had been. If they had wanted to engage with local restaurant owners or shopkeepers, these were not the places to go. The menu included a selection of Jamaican cuisine, and everything was delicious. But however hard Felicity tried to relax and enjoy this indulgent occasion, she was constantly aware that they were dining in the plantation owner's historic home on an old sugar plantation. What's more, apart from one exception, the wealthy diners were white and those attending to them were black. Slavery might have been abolished centuries ago, but somehow Felicity felt that the world still had a lot of matters to address. She decided to engage the charming receptionist in conversation about the plantation's history. But alas, that was not within the receptionist's brief. If she had felt any resentment about the past cruelties that had been imposed on her people, it was more than her job was worth to reveal it.

But Felicity and Alistair had made additional plans. They were, after all, 'enlightened tourists'. When all the other guests had flown, they planned to stay on in an adjacent town and, to that purpose, had rented a house for a week from Airbnb. When, on their last night within the confines of the resort, Felicity had mentioned this to their cook, he had looked astonished.

"Where you staying?" he had asked her.

Felicity had told him the name of the small harbour town where they had booked a house and he, she was absolutely sure, had covertly rolled his eyes.

They had arranged a week's car hire and travelled to the airport on a coach with the rest of the family to pick it up. The others were flying out that day. The driver spoke proudly of his island home as they travelled between the gated resort and the airport. But not a single passenger except Felicity had the courtesy to listen to him. The resort that they had stayed in may as well have been on Mars.

With a car now at their disposal, Felicity and Alistair were able to explore the Jamaican hinterland. As they climbed away from the coast towards the densely covered mountains of the interior, they passed many isolated homesteads. Traffic was rare on these minor roads, apart from the odd lorry that would speed past belching blue exhaust fumes, and the very occasional private saloon car. From time to time they would slow down to allow small flocks of foraging goats to pass by, while mean looking dogs with narrow faces would survey them curiously from the roadside. After a while the dense forest gave way to a vast sugar plantation, with its tall sword-like emerald leaves and dried flower spikes waving in the breeze. The crop seemed ripe for harvest but, as yet, there were no machines in sight. They were due to meet the caretaker of their lodging later that afternoon, so they decided to turn around and head back down towards the coastal plain. A stream of children were returning uphill from school now, all smartly dressed in white shirts and brown, blue and bottle-green school uniforms. They chatted to each other and waved and smiled at Felicity and Alistair as they climbed, each pupil bearing a laden rucksack on their back.

The rental house was pretty enough from the outside. But shortly after they arrived it became clear to Felicity why the hotel worker had reacted to their plans in that way. The inside was a disaster: it was ill equipped, sparsely furnished and uncared for. When trying to explore the town and buy some provisions, they had felt gauche and totally out of place. For once in their privileged lives, their white faces had stood out amongst a sea of brown, and they had felt unwelcome and uncomfortable. The next morning they decided to cut their losses and seek accommodation elsewhere. It was now evident that it would have to be in a place designed for tourists, so they booked into a beach-side guest house. Alas the beach offered pleasures that were not exactly orientated to the needs of a middle-aged couple. Felicity sat on a hotel sun bed and watched the waves, grimly trying to ignore the bartering and sex tourism that was going on around them. The final straw occurred late that night when an adjacent disco upped the volume and shook the foundations of their lodging for the following three hours. The hotel manager apologised as they signed out and sorrowfully reimbursed them, while vowing to continue his struggles with the disco proprietors.

"Right," Alistair said. "Leave it to me this time. I shall find us a nice quiet hotel where we will be able to relax and see out the remaining few days here in peace and quiet. And wherever it is, there will definitely be no discos, persistent hawkers or half-naked men riding on horseback through the waves, parading slightly different wares. Agreed?"

"Agreed." But when Felicity read the details of the hotel that Alistair had chosen for them, she could not keep quiet. "No way," she protested, "I refuse to stay in yet another resort belonging to an international conglomerate."

"Oh, come on Flic, be reasonable."

"You know as well as I do, Al, that they all pay their local staff a pittance. And where do the rest of the profits go?"

Alistair groaned. He had heard this all before.

"Not to Jamaica, that's for sure."

"I'm sure you're right, Flic, but come on hun—"

"And what's more I wanted to experience the 'real Jamaica', not to spend my time amongst Americans, Germans and fellow Brits."

But they had little choice, and at least this hotel was

quieter than the others.

On their last evening Felicity encountered a British man in the lift, accompanied by his two British children. He seemed delighted to meet her, wanting to know where she was from, and desperate to tell her about his own home town. When they stepped out onto the same floor, he lingered, wishing to prolong the conversation in his strong Midlands accent. His kids were young adults and he had brought them to Jamaica, he told her, in order to show them his country of birth. But it was clear to Felicity that he was feeling almost as much culture shock as she was.

Felicity
Albaygue Village, France
March 10th 2017

'La passion reste en suspens dans le monde, prête à traverser les gens qui veulent bien se laisser traverser par elle.'

– Marguerite Duras

The spring sun was already shining into her room as the radio came to life and Felicity began to stir. Today was her very own saint's day, 'le jour de Sainte Félicité'. But apart from the cat, there would be no one else to share it with her. Francoise Hardy was singing in her sultry voice as she forlornly walked the streets of Paris, 'sans joi et plein d'ennui'. But Felicity would have none of it.

"It's my saint's day today, Minou," she announced. "I think we should celebrate."

Minou was nestling in the crook of her knees, but he must have already known, for he had already left her a present of a tiny field mouse, deposited outside the patio door much earlier that morning.

"What shall we do?" she asked, as she rubbed behind

his ear. With a name like hers, she reflected, today should bring nothing but happiness. It was at this precise moment, as Minou ignored her and jumped down from the bed; as she was taking stock of how much her life had shrunk, that she was struck by a sudden *coup de foudre*. She determined there and then to tear up her roots in France and return to live in the UK. But why? Perhaps it had something to do with that lady in town yesterday who had asked her the way to the museum. When Felicity had started to explain, for the museum was one of her favourite haunts nowadays, the lady had abruptly cut her off.

"Pah! Anglaise!" she had spat, before turning away to ask someone else.

Was this the reason Felicity's passionate Gallic love affair had finally come to an end? No, it couldn't possibly be. Not for something as trivial as that. For sure, her French neighbours were friendly enough, and after more than two decades of living here, France had come to feel like her true home. So what on earth was going on? Felicity had fallen in love with France such a long time ago. As a schoolgirl, she had been entranced by the sexiness of French singers on the jukebox, and the scent of Gaulois in the air. The nature of her infatuation had changed, but it remained strong, cemented by many seasons of idyllic holiday wanderings with Alistair and their young family. At first they had camped, discovering the wildflower strewn plateaus of the Auvergne and the barren limestone causses and river gorges of the Languedoc. But as Alistair's job progressed, they would spend a month every year in a hotel in Biarritz or on the Cote d'Azur. So when Alistair had been made redundant from his high-powered job, they had chosen to retire to this quiet region in the south of France. Now, after his death, the home they had chosen together was the inspiration for Felicity's gentle progression towards old age. She loved her little stone cottage, hidden away in the vast dry landscape of the Midi. So why on earth did she suddenly want to leave it all behind? It would seem that her Gallic lover had lost his charms. This abrupt change of feelings, in inverse proportion to the length of her wooing, left her feeling discombobulated but determined to make the best of the challenges that lay ahead.

"C'est la vie, Minou," she shrugged, as Minou pleaded with her for some cat food. "It's over."

But when Felicity thought about it further, she realised that it was truly an awful time for this to happen. By leaving now she was going to throw up her hard-won rights as a long-term French resident.

"Bloody bloody Brexit," she cursed. "What on earth do they think they are doing?"

But, alas, she already knew that change was unavoidable. She may have loved France passionately, but like an inconstant lover, France had never truly loved her. She was a foreigner and always would be. However fluent her French, she only had to open her mouth and people's eyes would narrow. It was time for this 'outsider' to return home.

Decision made, Felicity began to trawl the internet, directing her mouse over the length and breadth of England in a quest to find a suitable place to settle. No point returning to the North. She had forsaken her origins long ago. Nor to London where she and Alistair had bought property, and her children had grown up. Her family was scattered world-wide now. She really didn't know where she belonged.

One evening she found herself on 'street view' wandering around her old haunts in the historic west country town of Dunborough. She had lived there briefly as a gauche young teacher. Now her cursor was jumping all over the screen, exploring anew the historic buildings and sweeping Georgian crescents that she had once known nearly half a century ago. She traced the route back to her old flat in that famous street. Yes! There it was hidden away below pavement level. How lucky she had been to find it back then.

Continuing around the elegant curve with its iron railings and stone portals, she began to trace her daily walk to school, via the adjacent park and then out towards the leafy suburbs. There were the very same gated houses she had passed every day, constructed well over two centuries ago from the local stone. Nothing seemed to have changed much, except for the large modern cars parked in every driveway, and the ubiquitous burglar alarms above every front door. Her attention now focused on one particular and familiar house, somewhat larger than the others. Its tall metal gates stood wide open, inviting her to proceed up its wide driveway.

"Drat!" Felicity cursed, as a large white cross jumped out at her from the screen like a silent guard dog preventing her from entry. "I was just wanting to see if it had changed much." She determined to go back there in person instead, when she returned to Dunborough. "Just let them try and stop me," she vowed. Felicity backed out, manoeuvred the cursor towards a nearby sign, and enlarged the print in order to read it out aloud. "'Greenfields Academy. Private school for children aged three to thirteen. Headmaster: John K. Tomkinson BA (Cantab)'. So that's how things are… a private school indeed." Felicity paused to contemplate for a second, before grumbling, "No surprise there then. Real estate like that is far too good for ordinary kids nowadays."

Felicity could barely sleep that night. Revisiting Dunborough had stirred up memories. It was as if her younger self had taken over her frail body, exhausting her with its energy, its dreams and its disappointments. As the morning sun rose higher, filtering through the half-open patio doors of her riverside cottage, her enthusiasm returned and she began to search for sites of West Country estate agents on the internet. After a while she paused to clean her specs. She spotted a blackbird fleeing from an olive tree with its booty, while a great tit called from an overhead branch.

"Teecha. Teecha. Teecha," it proclaimed.

The mimosa trees were now ablaze with blossom, so Felicity vowed to bring some inside later, and fill her home with its woody scents. Was she mad? Did she really want to replace this paradise for a home in misty grey England? But images of Dunborough kept returning as the day progressed. So much had happened in her life since those days. She had visited many countries; toured capital cities and explored small villages; trekked through snow and driven through desert; travelled by air and sea. And yet Felicity now felt drawn to that time when she had very little, save her optimism and naivety. Maybe, by returning, she would close the circle, and perhaps even rediscover something about herself. She decided to make a cup of Earl Grey tea, and then scroll through the property sites once more.

"Eureka! This is it." Felicity had no doubt whatsoever.

Minou looked up in alarm as his owner began to shout out the wording on the screen before her.

"'Avon Court: Phase Three of this Luxury Riverside Development in town centre historic building. Last two or three bedroomed apartments available. Prices from £650,000'."

She felt giddy with excitement. For didn't she know this very building? She often used to stroll along the riverbanks there, when she wanted to get away from the noise of the traffic. It had been a place to seek out wildflowers and water voles. She had even seen her very first kingfisher nearby: a flash of electric blue that had skimmed from one side of the river to the other like lightning.

"Perfect. It's absolutely bloody perfect," she whooped. Her heart was doing a thousand flips, warning her to calm down unless she wanted to face another visit to the 'cardio'. But she couldn't stop herself from reading on. "'Managed gardens; heated swimming pool; sauna; restaurant/bar and gym'." Then she hesitated as she learned that they were only offering a 99-year lease. "Oh, what the hell," she decided, "that will certainly see me out." But there were other possible pitfalls too. The Annual Service charge, for example, was sure to cost an absolute fortune. But she had made up her mind, so nothing was going to deter her. "This place is absolutely bloody perfect for me," she announced to the four stone walls of her French cottage. "I'm going ahead, whatever anybody says. I know I can afford it, so what the hell."

Felicity spent much of the remaining day poring over the promotional photographs. She realised that a large part of the building must already be occupied, so the unreal images of women like 'Stepford Wives' waving from balconies and wandering through the riverside gardens on the arms of smiling be-suited men looked rather silly. She was looking forward to meeting her actual neighbours and longed for real conversation at last, in which she wouldn't be struggling to find the right vocabulary. The internal photographs featured wide mahogany staircases, stylish furniture, and state of the art kitchens. As if to emphasise the exclusivity of this place, she noticed some original modern art displayed on the walls of the foyer, and a Picasso ceramic in a special display case at the foot of the main stairwell. Felicity loved Picasso and couldn't mistake his style. She also noted that some of the gym facilities would tax a fit twenty-year-old, but what did she care?

"Yes, yes, yes," she exulted as she imagined herself swimming up and down that shimmering pool and sweating in the sauna. And then she hesitated on reading out the caption at the bottom of the page: "'Exclusive residences for the over sixties'. Oh Christ!" Did she really want to live alongside other crumblies? It was bad enough ageing, but watching your frailties reflected in everyone else around you would be life-sapping. Then she started to list the positives to herself in an effort to revive her initial enthusiasm. "I'm going to use the swimming pool and gym every day and bloody well start a fitness regime… Jane Fonda eat your heart out."

Felicity had spent much of her time in France seeing England through the prism of her daily newspaper. The Brexit campaign had depressed her terribly and she couldn't help worrying that everyone she met in England from now on would be Europhobic. For sure it had been her own generation who had been most in favour of Brexit. But then she knew for certain that many of her old friends hadn't voted for it, so she just had to hope for the best.

"After all," she had said to herself, "if I can afford one of those apartments without holding secret offshore bank accounts, or possessing a school report from Roedean, then others can too. I'm bound to find one or two neighbours with something in common."

Felicity withdrew her finger from the cursor and fell into a deep reverie. She was in her early twenties once more, counting the days until her next payslip, and searching for a flatmate to help her share the rent. She hadn't been able to resist that flat. Its location alone in the middle of a stylish crescent had almost made her swoon. OK, so it happened to be in the basement, and pretty basic at that, but she had signed the rental agreement straight away, knowing that she would make it special. Inevitably, she had soon found that heating and furnishing it were hard to square with her teacher's basic salary, and had come to the conclusion that if she couldn't find a flatmate soon, she'd be relying on school dinners to keep her alive.

"Well, I can certainly afford this flat now, and I am damn well going to buy it," she said, slamming shut the lid of her laptop.

But, in reality, this provided Felicity with a terrible dilemma. For how could she, a self-professed socialist, indulge herself in this way while so many British people were suffering from enforced austerity? She was a 'baby boomer' for sure and had profited greatly from rising property prices. But she had become sick and tired of reading criticisms of her generation in the press.

"We knew hard times, too," she reasoned with herself.

Felicity rehearsed this argument many times in the weeks ahead as she secured her purchase and began to arrange her move. She decided to let out her existing home on the holiday cottage market, so the break was going to be a gentle one in the first instance. Even her cat, Minou, who barely spoke English, could stay behind.

Tina
Copse Hill Immigration Removal Centre, Central England
September 20th 2017

"Get off me. Don't touch me. Leave... me... alone." Tina summoned up every last bit of energy that she possessed to utter those last three words, shaking her arm free of the guard's pincer like grasp as he marched her along a white corridor. After spending so long in that dark minibus, the endless rows of buzzing ceiling lights were doing her head in. It must be late now.

She had left her city flat early that morning to keep her appointment at the police station, just like before, fully expecting to be home in time for lunch. But on this occasion it had been different. They'd put her in this minibus without so much as a by-your-leave. She seemed to have been travelling for hours, passing through town after town, and watching as the misty twilight began to creep around and envelop the remains of the day. Lights had come on in all the houses as if to drive away the September gloom. She had felt so alone and longed to join those families in their bright kitchens and living rooms. How she had come to find herself there God only knows, pinned in place by a mirthless man in uniform who seemed intent on staring out of the window on the other side of the bus. How rude of him to have ignored her completely. She was now feeling both angry and scared as this same man was opening a door and thrusting her into the room before them. It stank of fear. It was obvious that the single plastic chair in the middle was waiting for her, so Tina sat down, trying to keep her back straight and her dignity intact. The guard remained there beside her. There was an empty table in front of them and little else, save the bare linoleum floor, a grey filing cabinet and yet another waspish overhead light. She had seen so many similar scenes on the television, and it all led her to believe that she was about to be subjected to an inquisition. But why? She had never done anything wrong in her whole life. Her chest hurt, weighed down by an avalanche of suppressed sobs, and her limbs felt heavy. She wouldn't cry. No way was she going to break down in front of this rude oaf. She was old enough to be his mother. How dare he treat her like that? The door opened and a middle-aged woman rushed in.

"Right, let's get this over quickly," she barked. "It's nearly time for me to knock off."

Who was this angry person? Tina was now being made to place all her possessions onto the empty table in front of her. You might have expected a woman to be more civil, but this certainly wasn't the case here. Tina clutched her handbag to her chest. No one was going to have that. It was personal.

"Give that here, Grandma," the first guard threatened.

How dare he? Tina watched in despair as her mobile phone and other possessions were taken from her and an inventory made. It was now becoming very clear that this was some sort of prison, and that she wouldn't be seeing her daughter for some time. How she regretted not telling her about all of this when it first happened. About how she had lost her job because she couldn't produce the right papers. She wasn't illegal, Tina knew that she wasn't, but nobody would listen to her. Of course her daughter would have known what to do, she realised that now. But then she had enough on her plate already without having to take on her mother's problems.

"Anything in those pockets?"

Tina shook her head angrily. These stupid oafs could stuff their own pockets full of junk if they liked, but she knew how to keep her clothes looking smart. They were checking their list now to make sure everything on the table had been recorded. Tina began to think about her beloved granddaughter and tried to imagine what she would be doing right now. Maybe she was already tucked up in bed, enjoying her bedtime story. Or maybe she was sitting on the sofa watching her favourite DVD. She ached so much to see them both, to talk to her daughter and tell her everything. But how on earth could she do that when they'd taken away her phone?

"Name? Age? Address?" The woman was firing questions at her.

Tina must have answered automatically, although her head was spinning under all that bright light.

"Nationality?"

"British." Tina stated.

The man behind her laughed sarcastically.

"I'm British," Tina insisted angrily. "What else could I be? I've been British all my life."

*

It was little wonder that she couldn't sleep. Tina was racked with exhaustion, but her mind was racing through every possible explanation for what had come about. Nobody had warned her that this was about to happen. It had just come out of the blue. Hadn't she done exactly what they asked her to and turned up on time for her Home Office appointment at the police station, just like she always did? All of a sudden she was being treated like a criminal. The overhead light was bothering her. No matter that it had been dimmed slightly, it still went on buzzing like an angry hornet.

Tired of tossing and turning, she sat up and looked around the tiny room in which she had been placed. She wasn't alone. When she had been brought in, she had seen a figure hunched under the bedclothes on the

34

second bed. She could hear her now, quietly sobbing. There was a shower at one end of the room and a small loo. Such lack of privacy felt disgusting, but Tina got up reluctantly to have a pee. They had given her some sort of pyjamas and a change of clothes for the morning: clean underwear and a threadbare grey tracksuit were lying across the bottom of her bed. They repulsed her. Tina always liked to look smart, but her own clothes were already dirty and crumpled so what else could she wear? Apart from two beds and those basic facilities, the room was bare: white walls; plain white bed covers; bright white light; even the concrete floor was coated in thin white plastic. A drain in the centre of the room gave the whole place the appearance of a bathroom and, what's more, it stank. Her stomach lurched as if she was going to be sick. But there was nothing to bring up. She had rejected the supper that was offered to her.

"Illegal immigrant." Those were the words that had been thrown at her time and time again. That was why she got that letter telling her to report to the police station in Bristol. That was why they said she had no right to health care or benefits. They could stuff that. Tina was proud. She had fought hard and made a good life for herself. She had had a good job, paid her taxes regularly and was able to put something away every month. That is, until they decided that she had to provide them with documentation she didn't have. No one else she worked with was asked to do that. Why did they pick on her? She wasn't... she definitely wasn't illegal. Her mum had been telling her that all her life. Tina knew that she had an absolute right to remain.

She must have dropped off then, but it wasn't long before she was rudely awakened by two guards barging into the room and shouting at her neighbour to get up and collect her things. One threw the bedcovers back to reveal a young woman, no more than a girl really, cowering against the pillows and babbling in some unknown language. Her skin was smoother and darker than Tina's, and her sweat glowed in the artificial light.

"Get yourself dressed," the female guard ordered.

The male guard just stood there, which disgusted Tina greatly. Was there no dignity in this place? The girl crept off the bed, cowering slightly and whimpering. A black refuse bag was shoved into her hands and she was told to collect her things. She hid behind the grubby shower curtain to get dressed.

"Here give me that." The guard retrieved the sack and began to throw everything that she could find into it: bottles of shower gel; a hairbrush; clothing; and a tiny soft toy in the shape of a tiger which had been lying beside the pillow.

Tina regarded the male guard with disdain as he stood leering at them with his back to the door, a large silver key chain hanging from his waist. Wasn't he old enough to be this girl's father? He should feel utterly ashamed of himself. The girl screamed as they took her arm and pushed her through the doorway. Tina heard the word Heathrow as their footsteps grew fainter and fainter down the corridor.

"Rassholes," she yelled at the closed door.

Tina was called to breakfast an hour later. It dawned on her that she was free to move around within that area of the building, but every time she heard a key turn in a lock elsewhere, her stomach lurched anew. When she reached the dining room, she was assailed by the constant clatter of crockery and chatter of voices. It reminded her of school dinners, just about the only thing she had ever enjoyed at that awful school she had gone to. She collected her breakfast from a hatch and carried it towards the edge of the room where she could watch proceedings from an empty table. It felt pretty obvious what this was all about. Everyone who wandered about in supervisory role, bar one male guard, was white. All the others were black like herself. She noticed a small family group, the mother fussing about and attending to her children anxiously. How Tina ached to be with her own daughter and granddaughter right then. Barely finishing the bowl of cereal before her, she rushed out of the hall and, as soon as she reached her empty room, she collapsed on the bed. This time she sobbed for real.

Felicity
Dunborough, England
September 20th 2017

The train was pulling up alongside the platform at Dunborough Railway Station, but Felicity was staying put. Everyone else could go crazy, but she for one had more sense. Unfortunately, the man who had grabbed the window seat before her at Paddington had other ideas. He was now pushing roughly against her legs in his effort to escape.

"Ah the penalties of old age," she mused. "If we're not fanciable, we no longer count."

There was absolutely no way she was going to concede any space, so she sat tight and enjoyed watching him struggle. Was she feeling nervous? Not more than was to be expected, considering that her life had just been upended. No, she definitely wasn't nervous. It was just that she had decided to take her time, simple as that. It may feel like a lifetime since she'd last lived there, but they were hardly likely to have pulled down any of those wonderful Georgian buildings in the town centre, so finding her way from the station to her hotel should be a doddle. Felicity's neighbour gave another violent push in his efforts to extricate himself and his baggage, but she had closed her eyes. If he was trying to hassle an elderly lady, he had another thing coming. She'd be sitting tight until the rush died down.

She began to rehearse her route, as she had already done so many times while planning this new venture. Along past the old theatre, turn the corner to the assembly rooms, then continue until the municipal library. How she hoped they hadn't done away with that like so many authorities had. Then she would turn into that pretty cobbled lane lined with Georgian tea rooms; go past The Minstrel pub with its outside seating and stop for a second by the abbey just to check that the stone angels on the façade were still climbing towards Heaven. After that it was just a short walk down the road to that little public garden, where she would probably sit on a bench for a bit before searching for her hotel. She thought she knew roughly where it was. She used to take her washing to a launderette around there, although the area did look a bit more upmarket these days.

The train emptied and Felicity was soon following the last passengers towards the end of the station platform and negotiating her way through the automatic doors of Dunborough Railway Station. Surprise! It wasn't raining, and the sun was spreading an apricot glow amongst the clouds as it descended towards the encircling hills. On this mild September evening her adult life seemed to have turned a full and highly satisfactory circle.

*

Felicity's train had pulled out of the Gare du Nord in Paris at seven forty-five that morning, so when she was finally shown to her room at the Charter Hotel in Dunborough she immediately unzipped her leather boots, collapsed onto the bed and fell asleep. She had liked the feel of this hotel the moment she caught sight of its simple brick façade and stone pediment and, when the door opened onto the stylish Georgian style interior, she could see how tastefully it had been restored. Judging from the accents of her fellow guests at reception, Americans liked this place too. Her room was exactly as she would have wished, with its elegant drapes and sumptuous double bed. A pretty rosewood desk and wing-backed armchair were placed in front of an arched window with its view over the quiet street below, and Felicity noted that it would prove very useful over the coming days as she completed the formalities for her purchase. Most of her own furniture would remain at the cottage in France, but a few chosen possessions would be arriving in a few days' time to coincide with the completion date for her new home. However comfortable this hotel may be, she felt impatient for that day to arrive.

She woke around midnight. She had missed dinner and was feeling hungry. She had noticed a bar fridge earlier, discreetly placed behind a wooden panel in the corner of the room, so she decided to investigate it for snacks. There was sufficient light shining through a gap in the curtains, so she started to grope around in the dimness, shivering slightly. That was strange. Try as she might, she couldn't find it. Had she been imagining things?

"Why on earth don't they keep a modicum of heating on in these rooms at night," she grumbled to herself. "I'd forgotten how cold British autumns can be." Deciding that a glass of water from the bathroom would tide her over until breakfast, she pushed open the adjoining door and switched on the overhead light. "My God!"

Felicity could hardly believe what she saw in front of her. Shielding her eyes from the sudden glare, her mouth dropped open in stupefied amazement. The bathroom was illuminated by a single unshaded light bulb which hung from a fraying twisted wire in the centre of the ceiling. For sure, there was a bath, a toilet and a wash basin as could be expected. What she had not expected was the thick greasy layer of grime and limescale that encircled them all. What's more, in place of the customary row of free toiletries and fluffy white towels, she noticed a large rectangular block of Lifebuoy soap lying by the taps, and two striped, exceedingly grubby towels draped over the bath's perimeter. She wrinkled her nose at the smell and backed away. She was going to go down to see the night concierge about this right now.

Stumbling out of her room, she felt her way along the corridor towards the stairs that she had been escorted up only a few hours ago. It was even darker now. There was no sign of any fire safety measures or emergency lighting to show her the way. This was really so unexpected, she was going to have to complain vociferously, although she wasn't normally the type to make a fuss. By the time she had reached the end of the corridor, her feet had started to feel very cold, and she realised that she had forgotten to put on her boots. The jumper and skirt she had fallen asleep in felt inadequate and she was now shivering violently. She reached out to grip the railing that curved round at the top of the staircase in an elegant swirl, and cautiously began her descent. But the railing had obviously not been maintained properly and started to wobble. What's more she had felt sure that the stairs had been sumptuously carpeted, but now she felt the roughness of splintering wood snagging her stocking feet.

After negotiating the bottom stair, she turned away from the front door towards the reception area. But what a scene of devastation now met her. Strips of wallpaper were hanging from the walls and patches of damp leached through the exposed plaster.

"My God," she wailed, "this is unbearable."

A sudden noise broke the eerie silence of the chilly corridor. Felicity swung round to see the door slowly

42

opening. Daylight flooded in, revealing two small figures at the entrance. The first, a young boy, had his back to her and was pulling a large pram, shaped like a pudding bowl, up the stone steps and over the threshold. Guiding the pram from behind was a young girl. Felicity also noticed a third person standing in the shadows.

"Come on, Miss," the boy encouraged.

The figure, a youngish looking woman, hung back. She seemed reluctant to enter. By this time the children had managed to get the pram inside, half blocking the hallway. Felicity couldn't even see a baby, and very much hoped that it wasn't lying under the large black refuse sack which she deemed to be stuffed full of clean washing. Woollen jumpers, shirts, work overalls and large grey nappies all appeared to have been put in the wash together, and were now bursting from it in a tangled heap.

"It's all right, Miss. You can come in," the small girl wheedled with a pretty smile.

Her blonde hair looked tatted and her face bore smudges of dirt. Felicity felt a wave of emotion for these two children, and in her rush to protect them she completely forgot how angry she had been feeling. The figure behind them had vanished into the shadows and now Felicity seemed to be taking her place and was being shown into a small back kitchen.

"Here you are, Miss," the boy continued. "This is our kitchen. You can sit down there if you like." He proudly offered her a wooden chair. "Me and Lillian always does the washing at that launderette every Saturday to help our mam out. It's funny we never seen you there before." He was struggling with a large metal kettle and trying to fill it from the single cold tap at the Belfast sink. "Do you want a cup of tea? Get the mugs down, Lillian."

He started to bear the kettle over towards a greasy gas stove in the corner, and Felicity had to resist intervening as gouts of water slopped from the spout all over the stone floor. She doubted that the boy was old enough to handle a kettle of boiling water safely and declined with what she hoped was a kindly smile. What's more, those mugs that were now sitting beside a pile of newspapers and toys on the table didn't look too clean.

"No thanks, Albert. But it's very kind of you." My goodness, she already seemed to know his name: Albert, and Lillian his twin sister. How could she possibly know that?

"Our mam's at the hospital today cos she's not well. She had to take the baby with her in his pushchair," Albert continued.

That was something else she already knew. Oh God. Their mum was going to… Felicity closed her eyes. She couldn't bear to think of it. These poor, warm and generous children didn't deserve what was coming to them. Life just seemed so damned unfair.

The phone rang from her bedside table. It was reception with her wake-up call. Somehow, in the night, her world had been set to rights. She sighed with relief. Just a dream, thank goodness.

After a long hot shower, she was soon heading for breakfast. She salivated at the wonderful smells that rose up the stairwell from the dining room. Various members of staff passed her in the corridor. How welcoming everyone seemed. Had she slept well? Would she like them to get her a newspaper? Such warmth and friendliness. It reminded her of the English ticket collector yesterday who had been so full of bonhomie, you'd think she was his oldest pal. It was different in France, she reflected. Not that people were ever rude exactly, just slightly aloof, and it did take so much longer to gain their trust. It seemed to Felicity that British people expected you to share one's most intimate details the minute you'd been introduced. Maybe this wasn't such a bad thing after all, but she wasn't so sure. It was fair to admit that she was beginning to feel a little lonely in her French idyll. But as she was shown to her table, she cautioned herself to remain a little sceptical. Were these people really her friends? How could everyone be so warm and welcoming when over half of them had voted for Brexit? Or were friendly welcomes reserved for the select few?

Felicity was curious to learn a little more about the hotel, so after a restorative breakfast of bacon, eggs and somewhat inferior croissants, she sought out the hotel receptionist.

45

"I used to live here you know," Felicity told her. "Back in the early seventies. I know that's a bit before your time, but I was trying to remember if the Charter Hotel was here then."

"I'd love to help you," the receptionist gushed, "but I'll have to ask the manager what information he has. What I do know, though, is that this street used to be owned by the council. Apparently, it was a load of old slums, social housing, that type of thing. When they sold it off, our company bought up three houses in the terrace and converted them into this hotel."

"They've certainly done it beautifully… such a lovely hotel, so refined."

"That's really kind of you to say so." They shared a warm smile as Felicity thanked her and turned to go. "Don't hesitate to ask if there is anything else I can do for you," the receptionist added.

"Thank you so much. I certainly will."

As Felicity retreated back along the corridor, her smile vanished. Something about this hotel was making her feel uncomfortable. She hadn't slept well and had been troubled with dreams. Normally she would have stopped to study the portraits of elegant ladies and gentlemen who smiled down at her from the walls as she headed up the stairs, but she continued on, head bowed, failing to notice anything other than the patterns on the Axminster carpet. When she reached her room, she saw that the door was ajar.

"Oh my God, you didn't half give me a shock."

"Oh, I'm so sorry. I didn't realise…"

"I thought I'd just do your room while you were at breakfast. I hope that's all right."

"Of course, that's quite OK," Felicity said with a warm smile. "It suits me better actually, as I don't plan to go out until this afternoon. Thank you so much." She noticed that her smile was not reciprocated.

"I won't be long now. I'm nearly done."

Felicity noted the name tag pinned to the woman's nylon overall: she was talking to Gloria. She moved out of the way and watched from the corner of the room as Gloria finished smoothing the bed cover and proceeded to empty the bathroom rubbish bin into a black refuse sack.

"If you want to do it at the same time tomorrow, Gloria, that will be fine with me."

Gloria acknowledged this with a faint grunt, gathered up the rubbish sack and moved towards the corridor outside. Failing to close the door behind her she headed off towards the back staircase.

Felicity
The Charter Hotel, Dunborough, England
September 24th 2017

Felicity was used to finding Gloria in her room by now as she returned from breakfast. She had come to look forward to their brief chat, even though Gloria remained aloof and slightly cold. There was something about her that she liked, and although she barely knew her, there was something familiar about Gloria. Friendship and trust grew slowly in France, but in Felicity's view such beginnings often proved to be worthwhile. She had come to believe that if friendship is won too easily, it isn't worth a fig. This morning, when she reached the top of the staircase, she could hear shouting coming from further up the corridor, and as she approached her room, she saw the hotel manager standing in the open doorway with his back to her.

"How many times have I told you not to clean a room while the guest is at breakfast? They don't want to come back and find you still busy. It just isn't good enough."

"But, but…" Felicity heard Gloria plead.

"You'll just have to wait until they go out. There's plenty of other things to be done on this corridor. Have you stacked the linen cupboard recently? And that panelling could certainly do with a polish."

Felicity retreated slightly and hid around a corner until she could safely return to her room. Things grew quiet, but then the manager exploded again.

"Did you not hear what I said, woman? Don't clean the rooms when the guests are at breakfast... period."

There was a pause before Gloria responded. This time Felicity could hear her all too well.

"OK then, if that's the way you want it. You haven't even bloody well bothered to ask me my side of things. Don't expect to see me here tomorrow, because I'm never coming back."

Felicity waited until she could hear the manager's footsteps in the corridor as he headed for the back stairs. She slowly emerged from her refuge and, as she entered her room, she saw that Gloria was sitting in the wing chair with her head in her hands, sobbing. Felicity sat opposite her on the edge of the bed and waited in silence. Her own youngest daughter was probably of a similar age, and she had nursed her through some pretty stormy emotions.

As the sobbing subsided, she said quietly, "Would you like to talk?"

"No thanks, not really," Gloria sniffed.

She stood up and began to concentrate on gathering her things, all the time avoiding looking at Felicity.

"You sure?"

There was a pause as Gloria turned and assessed her coldly. "I'm all right," she assured her. "You get used to bastards like that. There'll be someone new cleaning your room tomorrow."

"I don't want someone else. I've enjoyed talking to you."

Gloria breathed in sharply. It was plain that she was struggling to hold back further tears.

"Have you got any kids?" Felicity asked.

"A little girl, she's nearly six." Gloria smiled fleetingly. "That's the problem. I'm always in a rush. It's Sunday today, and I've had to leave her at home on her own."

"Isn't there anyone else who can look after her?"

"Her nana normally comes up at weekends, but she's gone off the radar. Doesn't answer her phone. I've been trying to call her since Friday. There's also Winston, my son. He's eighteen, but he spends most of his time in Bristol nowadays."

"And now you've packed in your job. What are you going to do?" Felicity wondered whether she had gone too far. Gloria was obviously too proud to suffer prying. "You know I don't think I could stand your manager either. He's a right pri—" Felicity raised her eyebrows and left the last word hanging in the air between them.

Gloria got her drift and spluttered with disbelief. Then they both started laughing at the same time. Felicity was thinking rapidly now. She hardly knew this woman. So why on earth should she want to interfere? But she did know what it was like being a working mum. She had found life a struggle herself at Gloria's age, before Alistair's career had taken wing. She decided to try out a vague idea.

"Wait a bit," she pleaded. "Why don't you sit down for a second."

Gloria hesitated and then did as she was asked.

"I told you that I was only here for a week until I can move into my own apartment next Thursday, right?"

Gloria nodded suspiciously.

"Well, you've no doubt noticed that I am not exactly in the first flush of youth. I've got arthritis nowadays, and I can't do nearly as much for myself as I would like to." Gloria looked slightly bored, but Felicity decided to go on. "I'm pretty desperate to find someone to help me move in, but the trouble is I don't know a soul; it's been so long since I last lived here. The apartment is sort of a new build, so there's bound to be some cleaning up to do." Felicity noticed that Gloria was beginning to pay a little more attention so she decided to continue. "I've got some things arriving from France, so there'll be hanging pictures, arranging things, that sort of thing to do as well. And then there's the new furniture I've ordered. That will have to be assembled... never my strong point at the best of times."

Gloria groaned in agreement. "My God, you should see me with all those flipping bits and bobs. It takes me forever to get it right, and I always end up losing something."

Felicity felt encouraged. "How about I offer you a job helping me every morning? Just until you find something you prefer. Weekdays, so you can look after your little girl. What's her name?"

"Alice."

"No, I don't believe it. That's the name of my eldest."

"You got daughters?"

"Two. And a son. But I'm certainly not going to admit how old *he* is."

They both laughed.

"They live around here?"

"Sadly no. My son lives over in America."

"Oh." Gloria fell silent. "But your daughters will visit you surely."

"I suppose so, once in a while. My eldest lives up in Scotland, so it's a long way for her to come. As for my youngest, we were never really that close."

"I can't imagine not having my mum around," Gloria reflected. "Family's important."

Felicity persisted. "What do you think? About the job? Is it a yes?"

"Where you going to be living?"

When Felicity told her she raised her eyes to the ceiling and whistled.

"There's no way I could work there."

"Why on earth not?"

"Look," Gloria said. "I don't mean to be ungrateful or anything, but can you honestly imagine me going there every day to help you? Walking in through those great big front doors?"

"What do you mean?"

"I'm not being rude about you, believe me. You're all right. But everybody knows about that place. They're all stinking rich there."

"Hmm... I don't know about that. But why should that stop you anyway?" Felicity protested.

"There's a lot of talk about that place, and the people who live there. My friend's landlord does for a start. Apparently, he lives all on his own in some bleedin' great penthouse apartment, while he screws her for rent. She pays him an absolute fortune, and she hasn't even got a decent sized kitchen. It took him two bleedin' months to send someone to mend her boiler, even though she's got two small kids and the whole place was freezing."

Felicity sighed. What could she possibly say to that?

"Men like him don't want to see people like me hanging around their place, do they?"

"I still don't get it. What do you mean? You'll be helping me. It's got nothing to do with anyone else."

Gloria raised her forearm towards Felicity and pointed at it forcibly. "I'm black, aren't I?"

"What's that got to do with it?"

"Let me explain," Gloria said, sighing like a frustrated teacher. "This isn't London, or Birmingham or even Bristol for that matter. This is Dunborough."

"So?"

"You mean you haven't noticed? Have you seen many people like me around here? I bet you haven't."

"But Gloria. I really can't accept what you're saying. OK… I'll admit you know much more about this than I do, and I'm certainly not going to pretend that prejudice doesn't exist. But there are laws to protect you from that sort of thing. The Race Relations Act…"

"Pah! Try telling that to the Rasta guy who got tasered in the face by a cop in Bristol just for trying to go through his own gate. And he was a police race relations adviser." Gloria laughed ironically. "Honestly, you should try having a teenage son around here. I worry myself sick when I know Winston's going out with his friends in Bristol. You've heard of the 'sus laws', have you? They want you to believe that they're cutting back on it, but it's not true. Winston's a good lad, but what's that got to do with the price of cheese when he's black?"

Felicity felt sickened. Bringing up children was hard enough at the best of times. She couldn't start to imagine what it must be like for Gloria, even in this supposedly enlightened day and age.

"So you're going to let me down?" she said, putting on a petulant face in the hope of making Gloria smile. But that was never going to work. How stupid of her. Thoughts were coursing through the room, twisting and turning in different directions.

Felicity retreated to her past. She had been aware of some Afro-Caribbean children at her school in

Dunborough, but no more than two or three. She had been so naïve back then, so caught up with her own emotional awakening, that she hadn't really considered how they might be feeling.

Gloria was remembering her school days too. How she had stood out from the rest. Those bloody teachers just turned their backs on the insults and jibes she had to bear. It was just banter, everyone said, but it nearly destroyed her. She had toughened up since then; learned to cope. But certain places you just knew to avoid. The silence felt awkward, but each was reluctant to break it. Finally, Felicity took charge.

"Gloria." She paused to clear her throat. "I am probably as guilty as anybody when it comes to being insensitive about matters of race. I don't always get it right, I know that. And you know I need someone like you to point out where I go wrong." She noticed that Gloria was taking her seriously. "Look, if anybody tries to make you uncomfortable, then we'll just have to stand up to the bastard together, all right?"

Gloria took an intake of breath. Had she shocked her? Maybe older women weren't supposed to use words like that, even if she did.

"Excuse my French," Felicity continued, "but come on, Gloria, why don't we? If anybody tries to make life uncomfortable for you, we'll just tell them where to get off."

Gloria remained silent. She looked so solemn that Felicity began to feel nervous. A pigeon cooed gently from the rooftops as she waited for a response.

"Oh, all right then, I'll give it a go. But don't blame me for not warning you. You won't find all your neighbours are as generous as you."

"Generous? It's got nothing to do with being generous. I'm asking you to do me a favour, aren't I? And you know, Gloria, if you think about it, you're going to need a good up-to-date reference before you start looking for another job."

By now the pigeon had been joined by another, and they were becoming animated.

"All right then, I'd like to accept," Gloria announced. "When would you like me to start?"

Felicity
Avon Court, Dunborough, England
September 28th 2017

The removal van had been and gone, leaving Felicity
with a mass of boxes, bundles and cases lying on the
fitted carpet in front of her, and a stack of framed
pictures leaning against the newly painted walls. The
driver and his mate had claimed to be in a hurry, but at
least they agreed to position what little furniture she had
brought over in its rightful location. This included a
three-quarter lit bateau which would take pride of place
in the spare bedroom, and her little French walnut
writing desk from which she could not bear to be parted.
It wasn't really appropriate for this apartment, so she
decided to use the spare bedroom as a study. It would be
her little French retreat. As for the rest of the flat, she
favoured a minimalist style, taking advantage of the
light that flooded into the lounge from the patio
windows and balcony beyond. She would retain the
basic off-white walls and create a small gallery with her
favourite pictures and posters. Not original, of course,

but gleaned from her many visits to French galleries over recent years. The one original landscape oil painting that she possessed, and valued above all, was to hang in her retreat/study. As for the hundreds of books that were waiting to see the light of day, they would have to wait a bit longer until the bookcases she had ordered could be assembled. Kindles were all very well, but Felicity did like to be surrounded by books. What on earth was she going to do if Gloria failed to turn up? She realised that she was really going to be quite dependent on her for a while.

"Oh good. That must be her," said Felicity as she crossed the room to authorise Gloria's entry from her door phone. Shortly afterwards there was a faint rap and she looked up to see her new assistant standing on the threshold to her apartment. It was ten o'clock on the dot, just as had been agreed.

"Hiya," Gloria called.

What a transformation. She had looked so severe, dressed in that horrid nylon chambermaid's uniform, with her hair scraped back from her brow into a tight ponytail. Now that her curls hung loose and full about her face, she looked altogether more carefree. Dressed in slim coloured jeans and a smart denim jacket, she seemed so much younger too.

"Am I glad to see you," Felicity announced. "As you will notice from the chaos around you, they've already been and gone."

Gloria was holding her jacket in front of her and

seemed to be wondering where to put it.

"Why don't you leave that on the bed in the spare bedroom over there. By the way, are you any good at putting up coat hooks?"

"You wanna bet." Gloria grinned. "I'm the all-time expert. I haven't been a single parent all these years without learning to do things for myself. Now, what do you want me to do first?"

Felicity directed her towards some boxes bearing the inscription: CROCKERY, CUTLERY, GLASSES. "You can start unpacking those into the kitchen cupboards if that's OK with you." The kitchen formed an extension off the main lounge. It was, as they called it in France, 'une cuisine americaine'.

"Wow, I like this." Gloria was running her hand over the marble kitchen counter and looking enviously at the fitted appliances.

It made Felicity feel slightly uncomfortable. She herself would have once found such luxury a little over the top, especially for one person. However, she was delighted that things had got off to such a good start. Somehow Gloria's edgy persona had been left behind at the Charter Hotel.

That evening Felicity decided to try out the swimming pool. As she stepped towards the lift that would take her down to the basement, she nearly collided with another lady of a certain age who was stepping out. It was evident from her damp blonde hair and fluffy towelling robe that this was a fellow resident returning from her swim.

"Oh hello," she said. "You must be the new occupant of Flat 8. I'm Joan from Flat 2." She offered her a limp well-manicured hand, resplendent with scarlet nail varnish. "I'm living along the corridor from you. I gather you've just moved in."

The doors closed just in front of them and Felicity watched as the lift departed without her.

"Oh, er… er… yes. How do you do? I'm Felicity. People know me as Flic."

"How are things going? If you need anything, you know where to find me now. Don't hesitate to knock on my door."

Felicity smiled gratefully while trying to assess this lady's age. Not young, but certainly very well preserved. But still, she seemed friendly enough. So much for Gloria's scepticism.

"I bought my flat when they were selling phase two," Joan continued. "They hadn't even started renovating your wing. Gosh, it's hard to believe I've been here for six months already." She touched Felicity's arm lightly. "I must say it's a very friendly place. I do hope you'll be happy here."

"Well… yes," Felicity demurred. "Thank you." She edged closer to the lift doors, but her new neighbour seemed to want to continue.

"I know it's early days, but you might like to think about joining us on the 'Residents' Committee'. I would welcome a bit of support on the female side. These men do tend to dominate the proceedings, especially the Colonel." With this, she gave an exasperated look up the wide mahogany staircase towards the top floor and raised her eyebrows.

Felicity smiled in complicity, while wondering what that was all about.

"Still, I see you're going for a swim. I'd better not stop you. It's twenty-seven degrees today. Not bad... but I do wish they'd keep it a little warmer. None of us are getting any younger here."

After making her escape, Felicity located the basement changing rooms, which appeared to serve both the pool and gym facilities, and after quickly changing into her bathing suit, she was soon lowering herself into the pool with a long and grateful sigh. She was totally alone, and the slightest noise reverberated around her as if she were in an empty theatre. After swimming a few leisurely lengths, she turned over to float on her back. There was a faint hum from the overhead lighting, while water gurgled gently in the adjacent Jacuzzi. She was determined to swim here daily; it felt so relaxing. She would buy herself a towelling robe too, like Joan's, which would make the process even easier. As she reflected on her first day, she wondered whether she felt any regrets about her move. At that particular moment, she couldn't think of a single one.

Tina

Copse Hill Immigration Removal Centre, Central England

September 29ᵗʰ 2017

Tina had slept fitfully that night and was now lying on her back staring at the cheap plastic lamp above her head which still emitted a constant buzz. Her new companion snored gently on the other side of the narrow room. Without any natural light coming in, it was hard to gauge the time, but the corridor was silent. Much against her will she had begun to get used to the routine and was waiting to hear people moving about so that she might think about getting up for breakfast. What use was there in continuing to fight this? She had cried and cried and felt utterly exhausted. There was some relief now in sharing stories with others and trying to bring comfort where she could. Surely before too long someone would realise that this was all a stupid mistake and send her home?

The door opened abruptly and two guards barged in.

"I want you to get up and get dressed now, Mrs

Gayle," the female guard barked.

Tina regarded this woman's male companion with suspicion as she waited for him to turn away, but he seemed oblivious to her concerns.

"Hurry up now," the guard insisted, "if you want to have any breakfast before we leave."

"Where are we going?" Tina asked hopefully. It was about bloody time they put this thing right.

"Heathrow, dear," the male guard condescended, his lip twitching slightly. "I believe it's nice and sunny in Jamaica."

Tina's screams echoed around the room. They bounced off the ceiling and burst through the open door. By now every single person along the corridor who had actually managed to get some sleep was lying wide awake.

Felicity
Avon Court, Dunborough, England
September 29th 2017

Gloria arrived shortly after nine the following morning. They had agreed she should work all day as there was still much to do before the furniture delivery on Monday, and Gloria needed to stay home with Alice over the weekend. Felicity had winced as Gloria hammered in the first picture hook. But she did it well, and before long they had arranged some of her favourite pictures along the side walls.

"Do you really like this Picasso?" Gloria asked, looking slightly pained.

"Well yes. I wouldn't have chosen it otherwise," Felicity protested. "Why? Don't you?"

"Not much. He was a bit of a bastard towards his women, wasn't he?"

Felicity laughed. "But that doesn't make his work any less worthwhile. Why don't you like this one?"

"It's a bit… I don't know… a bit too abstract. I prefer his earlier works." She suddenly brightened. "*Child with a Dove*. Now that's lovely… more straight forward."

Felicity nodded in agreement.

"But if I had been one of those beautiful women sitting for him, I'd have hated the way he twisted my face about. He makes them look so ugly."

"Well, I do see what you mean." Felicity laughed. "But I still maintain that he was a genius. What do you think of his lovely ceramic bowl in the entrance hall? Do you like it?"

"You're kidding me. That's not really a Picasso, is it?"

"They tell me it's genuine. It's very like what they call a 'tauromache' in France, one of a series of ceramics that he created with illustrations of bullfighting, because every bowl was curved like the arena."

"How clever!"

"Each scene was a little bit different. I used to love going to the museum in Céret to see them."

"Are they all gruesome like that one downstairs? I'm not sure I like the idea of bullfighting really."

Felicity realised that Gloria must have paused on her walk inside to look at the lovely bowl. This pleased her enormously. "I know just what you mean. I'm afraid he did seem to enjoy depicting bulls and matadors, but then I suppose he was Spanish after all."

"True," Gloria conceded.

"I guess our bowl was done a bit later than the tauromaches. Do you know, he didn't even start to get interested in ceramics until he was over sixty."

"It's not too late for you then, Flic. You'll have to join a local pottery class."

"You know, Gloria, I'd love to. Why don't you come too?"

Gloria laughed. "That's not such a bad idea."

"But no, Picasso's ceramics were certainly not all gruesome. He had great fun making all sorts of images – goats, women, fish, you name it. And not just bowls either – jugs, vases, plaques, bottles. Oh it was all such great fun, and quite ground-breaking."

"Wow," Gloria exclaimed. "Mind you, I would never have believed that one downstairs was a real Picasso. It just looks like it was painted in a mad dash." She paused, before adding cynically, "It must be worth a lot of money nowadays though."

"Well, let's just say 'best not eat your cornflakes off it'. Tell me, Gloria, if you're not too keen on Picasso, which artists do you like?"

"Mary Cassatt," Gloria responded instantly. "She's my favourite. I went to an exhibition of her paintings once when I was on holiday in France with my school. Anyone can understand what her pictures are all about: children, gardens, gentle and beautiful things."

Felicity remained silent as she busily rifled through the pictures that remained stacked against the wall. Pulling a small portrait from amongst them, she turned around and held it up towards Gloria. "Ta dah!" she exulted.

"Yes, I know it," Gloria shrieked.

They both considered the portrait of a young girl that Felicity was holding aloft, and for a moment nothing was said. Like many of Mary Cassatt's works it was a simple yet beautiful painting in predominant hues of grey and cream. She had painted a serious, rosy-cheeked girl, no more than eight or nine years of age, who stared pensively into the distance with her hands entwined and a large straw hat perched on her head. It was one of Felicity's favourites, and reminded her of Alice, her eldest daughter.

"I'm sure I saw that at the exhibition," Gloria said at last. "It's really lovely, isn't it? Do you know, Flic, how unusual female impressionist painters were?"

"Well of course, that's not surprising really," Felicity replied. "It was only the privileged and well-to-do who could afford to paint. Women were always going to be pushed aside."

"What about Van Gogh?" questioned Gloria. "Didn't he have to struggle?"

"OK, I suppose Van Gogh was an exception," Felicity admitted grudgingly. She was surprised by this conversation and struggled not to show it. Felicity prided herself on her liberal views, but she had caught herself out this time fair and square. What grounds did she have to believe that Gloria would not be able to hold her own when talking about art? Because she was a chambermaid? Maybe, Felicity worried, she was just as prejudiced as all the rest.

Gloria was now rifling around in the box of picture hooks for a missing tack. It would be interesting to ask her what she felt about the way portraits of successful white people dominated Western art. After all, Mary Cassatt was hardly any different. Surely Gloria must have been aware of this at the exhibition. No, Felicity decided, it would be better not to ask. It was true that Gloria had been the first to introduce the subject of race, but she was terrified of causing offence. Would that, she wondered, count as inverted racism?

"Did you enjoy art at school?" Felicity asked tamely.

"Loved it. Actually, it was my best subject. I even got a decent result at GCSE."

"So you liked school?"

"Nah. I was generally pretty hopeless, messed around too much."

"That's a pity. I bet you could have done well."

Gloria's eyes narrowed as she assessed Felicity anew. "You sound just like a teacher."

Felicity just laughed as Gloria continued.

"My mum hated school too. But then she went to a real dump. At least she ended up with some decent qualifications in later life. Not like me."

"How come?" Felicity was watching Gloria now as she climbed the stepladder with the picture hook wedged between her lips and a hammer in her hand. "Careful now."

"Will this do just here?"

"Up a bit and to the right. OK, stop right there."

Gloria successfully positioned the picture hook and banged it in.

"Well done."

She stepped back down to the floor and rested the hammer on top of one of the many unopened boxes. "Dad walked out when I was very small. That's what got her going. My nana originally came over here to be a nurse but she gave it up for a bit to look after me so my mum could go to college."

"Maybe it's not too late for you to do the same, Gloria."

"Nah. There aren't the same opportunities anymore. Not like there were back then. And anyway, I couldn't take on any more debt."

Felicity had to acknowledge that Gloria was probably right about that. It was criminal the way that adult further education had been shrunk. She herself had not been very diligent at school and had got much more out of studying as a mature student. And for her it had all been entirely free. But she decided it was time to shut up about the subject or she might reveal too much about herself. She understood only too well why people like Gloria hated teachers and, besides, she had left that episode of her life way behind. Was she even the same person as that foolish overconfident young teacher who came to Dunborough all those years ago?

"Time to stop for a bite to eat," Felicity announced. "I'm going to investigate that pizza place around the corner. Fancy some?"

"Not half."

"Did you happen to see the corkscrew when you were unpacking everything?" Felicity called from the doorway. "There's a nice bottle of rosé chilling in the fridge. Why don't you open it before I get back, and you can help me celebrate moving in? I assume you know where you put the glasses."

Felicity was away some time. There had been someone ahead of her in the queue at the pizzeria who was buying enough to feed an army. When she arrived back, she pushed the door open and walked towards the kitchen counter to deposit the boxes and find some plates. Gloria was nowhere to be seen. Then she heard a low and urgent voice coming from the spare room.

"Mum, it's Gloria. Where the hell are you? I've been trying to get you all week. Why didn't you come up last weekend as usual? I've promised Alice we can all go shopping tomorrow. She's missing you, Mum. Please ring me back as soon as you get this." There was a pause. "Please!" she repeated in a low and urgent voice. "Love ya."

Felicity coughed and clattered two plates down onto the counter. After a few seconds Gloria emerged from the side bedroom.

"Oh sorry, I didn't realise you were back. I was just getting something from my bag." She blew her nose and stuffed the tissue into the pocket of her jeans. "I opened the wine," she continued, going over to the fridge and holding it aloft. "Confession!" she giggled. "I had a little sip."

They laughed conspiratorially as Felicity began to pull open the pizza cartons and Gloria poured the wine.

"I don't know about you, but I'm starving. This one's chorizo and the other's a margherita, just in case you're vegetarian."

"I'll eat anything. I'm not fussy. By the way, I came across a pizza wheel earlier. I'll find it for you."

They walked towards the open patio doors, each balancing a plate of pizza and a glass of wine. There was still some warmth from the autumn sun, so they ate lunch while perching on the edge of some built-in ornamental flower troughs.

"That's something else I'm going to have to order…" Felicity commented. "Patio furniture."

They ate in silence while their diverse thoughts rose above the balcony, fell towards the river and were caught up in the rush and swirl of the cascading weir.

"Back to work," Felicity announced. "Let's see if we can finish hanging those pictures today. Hopefully, we'll be able to start assembling the bookcases on Monday, that is assuming they are delivered on time."

"I hope I can hang them straight," Gloria giggled. "I think I've had too much wine."

She was about to climb back up the stepladder when her phone rang.

Tina
Crook House, Heathrow Airport Immigration Removal Centre, England
September 29th 2017

It was taking forever for her to answer the phone. Where was she? Where *was* she? Tina's heart was pounding against her chest, and she wondered how much more stress she could endure before she passed out.

"Come on, baby love, pick up the phone," she pleaded. "Come on…"

"Hello? Mum, is that you?"

Thank the Lord her daughter was there at last.

"Mum, why haven't you been answering me? Didn't you get my messages?"

All the words that Tina wanted to say to her beloved daughter became jammed in her throat, and she just let out a long wail.

"Mum, Muma baby, what's happening? Where are you? And where the hell have you been? I've been ringing and ringing all week."

Tina was sobbing now.

"Muma, Muma, it's all right. Please don't cry. You're talking to me now. If you tell me what's wrong, we can sort this out."

Tina took a long shaky breath. "They told me I was an illegal immigrant and I couldn't work no more. I lost my job honey."

"What the f—"

"They made me report to the Home Office at Bristol Police Station. I've been doing it for a while. I know I shoulda' told you honey but…" She let out another long wail.

"But… they can't do that to you, Mum. You're not illegal. Oh my God, why didn't you just tell them? And why on earth didn't you tell me. Look, where are you? I'll come and get you right away."

"You can't honey," Tina wailed. "I'm a long way away. It's where they take you before they put you on the plane. That's…" She tried to catch her breath. "That's why they've returned my phone. They're sending me back to Jamaica."

Felicity
Avon Court, Dunborough, England
October 4th 2017

Gloria didn't finish hanging the pictures that Friday. She left shortly afterwards, apologising profusely but without giving any explanation for her sudden departure. Felicity had remained tactfully silent, having heard enough through the narrow walls to know that the person on the other end of the phone was desperately upset.

"Look, I'm sorry to let you down like this," Gloria had mumbled.

"Please, Gloria, you really don't need to apologise. You've obviously got a lot on your plate. Look, you've been a great help these past couple of days, and it would be nice if you could come again. Just give me a ring when you can." Felicity had reached out to seal what felt to her like a new friendship, but stepped back, repelled by a barrier of tension.

The partial delivery of furniture arrived on Monday as scheduled. Her new mattress was now leaning against the wall of the master bedroom until the accompanying structure could be assembled. As for the bookcases, they lay in large rectangular boxes around the lounge floor. It was much too difficult for Felicity to assemble them on her own, but she set about unpacking her books and planning how they would be arranged. She was also going to need a dining table and chairs, and of course a sofa, which she planned to position with a view over the river. But Felicity had delayed ordering these until she got to know her new apartment. Now she felt absolutely certain that her original gut feeling had been right: minimalism would be the order of the day. But how was she going to achieve all this? If Gloria didn't contact her by the end of the week, she would have to go about finding someone else to help her.

On the Wednesday of the following week, Felicity heard a knock on the door. When she answered, she saw Joan standing there. Her hair was now a greyish-blonde and immaculately coiffured.

"I just wanted to say hello," she chirruped. "See if there was anything I could do to help." It was clear by the way she peered around and beyond Felicity that she hoped to be invited in.

"Can I offer you a cup of coffee?"

"Oh, how lovely." Joan pushed her way inside and then paused to look around. "Oh… gosh…" she wavered. "I imagine you must still be expecting some more furniture. I've heard you're moving from France."

Felicity laughed apologetically. "You're quite right.

I'm afraid I can't even offer you anywhere to sit at the moment." She was looking around the room frantically, trying to assess whether Joan would be comfortable sitting on one of the boxes. "Oh yes, of course I can. Aren't I silly?" With that Felicity barged into the spare bedroom and retrieved the single antique chair that she had brought over from France. It was a perfect match for her walnut desk, and she placed it in front of Joan. "Please, do sit down and I'll make us a coffee. Black? Sugar? How do you like it?"

"Oh, what a lovely chair," Joan gushed.

"Coffee?" Felicity insisted.

"Oh, er... yes please...white would be really lovely...with two sugars."

Felicity reflected how different people's tastes could be, as she set about operating her new in-built espresso machine. She wondered whether she would ever feel truly at home in England again. Who were these strange people who adulterated their coffee, poured milk in their tea and voted for Brexit? Or was she just bitter, like the dark espresso she was balancing in her other hand?

"Here you are," Felicity offered. "One white coffee, two sugars. You can rest it on top of that cardboard box."

The sunlight was streaming in through the patio doors, reflecting off the hard surfaces. Felicity couldn't help noticing Joan's barely concealed astonishment as she surveyed the empty room. It was clear that she was rather taken aback by the sparseness of it; the gallery of pictures providing the only decoration.

"Such a beautiful chair," Joan repeated. "I imagine you must be bringing more lovely French antiques over soon."

"Oh no. I have brought one or two older pieces over, but they are strictly for my little French boudoir." Felicity gestured towards the bedroom. "As for the rest of the apartment, I'm planning to furnish it in a more modern style."

Joan took a rapid sip of her coffee, as if to hide some confusion. "I just thought… given the historic nature of the building…" She paused. "Well, it is your flat after all."

The conversation turned to the 'Avon Court Residents' Committee'. Joan was keen to nominate Felicity, and proceeded to tell her about the other members, filling her in on the issues that had concerned them to date. Apparently one resident was putting out bird seed in order to attract wild birds to his balcony. This could had caused great upset among the residents as the birds created stains on the beautiful stonework. It was generally agreed that pets should not be allowed either. Joan planned to raise the topic of increasing the pool temperature, and hoped that, if Felicity were approved, she would support her in this. The other members were very pleasant people she assured her, although the Colonel did get a bit bolshie at times.

"I tell you what, my dear," Joan confided. "If you would like to come back to my flat with me, I'll find the proposal form for you. Thank you so much for the coffee. It was a real treat."

Felicity duly followed her neighbour along the quiet corridor.

"I'd love to invite you in but I've got a hairdressing appointment soon."

She disappeared inside to retrieve the form, leaving her newest neighbour on the threshold staring into a dark, heavily furnished room, wherein a clock steadily marked the passing of time. Felicity noticed how the long drapes not only shut out the light, but hid what must have been a wonderful view of the river below.

"Here you are, dear. I'm afraid I must rush, but if you could sign it and give it back to me, I'll do the necessary."

As Felicity returned to her apartment, she reflected that Joan's hairdressing bills alone would bankrupt a British state pensioner. But once inside she was hit by the sudden emptiness of the scene before her. It had been nice of her new neighbour to make overtures, and now Felicity was feeling remiss for thinking so churlishly. She picked up her mahogany chair to return it to the study, then sat down on it heavily and slumped forward at her desk, head in hands. She remained there agonising for some time. Felicity definitely did like her own company, she knew that. She always had. But it would be nice to have more contacts over here; after all, wasn't that why she had returned here in the first place? So why on earth couldn't she seem to warm to Joan's neighbourly overtures? She had always liked her French neighbours, but there had been a limit to what she could talk about with them, however friendly they were, when she struggled to find the right word or decipher a fast-flowing sentence. She could see frustration in their eyes too.

Since Alistair had died, the countryside that they had both come to love had been her chief solace, and Felicity looked up now towards their cherished painting of the Midi that hung above her temporary bed. How she missed the dry solitary landscape, represented here in shades of mauve, orange and brown. How she longed for distant vistas planted with row after row of vines and silvery green olive groves. And oh, what wouldn't she give to look out once more towards those sheer limestone cliffs that dominated her erstwhile home, where rivers and small waterfalls gushed from subterranean caves to meet and track their way along the valley floor. Her thoughts shifted, and she began to reflect on how nice it would be if one of her children would ring to see how she was. Alice had promised to visit her soon from Scotland, but so far there had been no commitment, and she was beginning to feel both unloved and neglected. At that precise moment her mobile phone rang and she rushed into the lounge to find it.

"Hello, Flic, it's Gloria."

"Oh hi. How are you?"

"I'm fine. Would you like me to come again

tomorrow, or have you found somebody else?"

"No, no I haven't. Look, I'm really glad you rang. Tomorrow would be great. I wanted to finish hanging those pictures myself, but I'm too nervous on those stepladders nowadays. You can resume where you left off."

Gloria arrived at nine fifteen the next morning. Alice's school wasn't too far away, so she had come straight there after dropping her off. At first she seemed rather stiff and embarrassed, but before long she was climbing the stepladder and commenting on the pictures as they were produced for hanging.

"This is the very last one." Felicity held up a large art gallery poster which featured one of Matisse's cut out pictures of a female nude. "What do you think?"

"It looks nice. I like that shade of blue. But I don't really get why he did so much of that kind of thing, instead of using paint," commented Gloria. The picture hook was already in the wall; she leaned forward to take hold of the frame and turned to put it in place. "Is it level?"

"Perfect," Felicity said.

Gloria climbed back down and stood to admire her morning's work. "I remember we were expected to cut or tear up paper to make collage pictures at school, but my God, they never looked like that."

Felicity was recalling how she had often given a similar task to her pupils. What a long time ago it all seemed to her now. "That's funny," she said. "I remember I used to give out coloured sticky squares of paper and scissors to kids and tell them to make a picture. I think it must have been the fashion in schools back then." What had she said? It was clear that Gloria had twigged, as she spotted her covertly rolling her eyes. "Of course, that was in a completely different era," she added quickly. Felicity went to the fridge and pulled out half of a homemade quiche and a bag of washed lettuce. "If you can stay on for a bit this afternoon, I could offer you quiche and salad for lunch. Then we could make a start on the first bookcase." She also pulled out an opened bottle of Sauvignon blanc which she waggled in the air with a questioning look.

"Not bloomin' likely. Sorry, I didn't mean to be rude, but the last time I was here it made me a bit squiffy."

"Yes, I know. I probably drink too much after all those years in France," Felicity confessed. "No one would ever dream of having lunch without a glass or two of wine over there. You know, we even used to see the local gendarme drinking wine with his lunch at our local café once upon a time."

It was too cold to sit outdoors, so they pulled some boxes in front of the patio doors, allocating one as a table. "Thank you," Felicity said simply, as she set down the plates before them.

"What do you mean?"

"Just thank you. I was beginning to feel a bit lonely and your coming has cheered me up."

They both started to eat and sip from glasses of

sparkling water that Felicity had also carried over. A rare chink of sunlight caught Felicity's blue Italian tumbler, causing her to recall that last trip to Venice when she and Alistair had chosen those glasses together. Gloria finally broke the silence.

"Flic... do you think I could ask you a favour?"

"Certainly, what is it? I'd love to help if I can."

"Mum and I have got an important meeting with a lawyer in Bristol the week after next, and it's half-term. Winston's working, and I don't know what to do with Alice."

"Are you asking me to look after her? If you are, I'd absolutely love to. You do realise I haven't even met her yet."

"Are you sure? The meeting is at eleven on Tuesday, so I'd have to bring her round about nine fifteen. You don't have to worry about entertaining her. She's heavily into 'Worst Witch' stories at the moment. You won't hear a peep out of her."

"Am I sure? If Alice is as nice as her mum, it'll be a pleasure."

Felicity wondered whether she had overdone it when she noticed Gloria brush away a tear. She decided to carry their plates back to the kitchen to give her friend a moment to recover. While she was there, she made them each a coffee.

"Have I remembered right?" she asked when she returned. "Black, no sugar?"

But Gloria didn't seem to hear. She was sitting with

her head bowed, staring fixedly at the carpet. Finally, she spoke. "The bastards," she said vehemently.

Felicity paused. Then she lowered the two coffee cups gently onto the box, resumed her place, and whispered, "Don't let your coffee get cold."

Gloria sipped tentatively.

After a while Felicity spoke again. "What bastards are those?"

"The bloody British Home Office that's who." There was another long silence before Gloria spoke again. "Do you know, Flic, when it was my mum came over here from Jamaica? Back in nineteen bloody sixty-eight, that's when. That's nearly fifty years ago... fifty bleedin' years. Wouldn't you say that that makes her British?"

"Yes, Gloria. I would say there's no question that your mum is British."

"What's more, my nana worked her arse off as a nurse for your country."

At that moment Felicity would have been very happy to disown her country, or Gloria's for that matter, but she remained silent.

"So what do they do? They tell Mum that she is here illegally and she has six months to get out. And you know, Flic? She didn't even tell me. All this time and I didn't even know."

"But why, Gloria? Why on earth did they say that?"

"She'd worked for this company for twenty years. It was a great job, lots of responsibility. Then thanks to this bleedin' government and their so called 'hostile environment', they had to go and ask her for paperwork to prove that she had a right to be here. She'd never even applied for a passport, nor nothing official like that, so she couldn't think what on earth to give them. So they said they weren't allowed to employ her any more... simple as that. After all that service she'd given them. Honestly, Flic, it makes my blood boil."

"And you didn't know anything about it? When did all this happen?"

"Six bleedin' months ago." Gloria caught a tear and smudged it against her nose. "And all this time I knew nothing about it. When she applied for unemployment benefit, they told her she wasn't entitled to it, nor health cover neither. If it hadn't been for her savings..."

"My God. How awful. How did you find out about all this?"

"Funny thing is, I'd suspected for some time that something was wrong. She's been edgy and losing weight. Then, unbeknown to me, she goes to report to them as usual... apparently that's what she's been doing all this time... and they goes and takes her away in a prison van without telling a soul. My mum, who's never done anything illegal in her whole life."

"My God I feel so ashamed. But at least she's back with you now, safe and sound."

"Oh no... not flippin' likely. She's back for now, but they're still saying she hasn't got the right to remain. She's terrified that they're going to take her away and that she'll never see us again. She's round at my place now. She hardly eats, and I know she lies awake at night crying. Can you imagine what it's like? Honestly, Flic, I had to come round here to get away from it all."

"God, I wish I knew how to help you. I feel so ashamed."

"Don't worry, Flic. It's not your concern. I shouldn't really be involving you like this."

"Gloria, you have to talk about it with someone, for your own sake. I just can't imagine how terrible it must be for you all."

"I've got in touch with the Refugee Council now. They seem to know all about this sort of thing, and they're really supporting us. And thanks to them our local MP is on the case too."

"Oh, that's good to know… surely—"

"But, you know, Flic, I'm still so afraid for her. If she's forced to return to Jamaica, before we can do anything to stop them, she won't have a penny to her name. I just can't imagine what it would be like to be somewhere where you don't know a soul."

"I went to Jamaica for a holiday once. I don't mean to alarm you, Gloria, but your mum would find it very difficult to fit in. Of course, it must have been very different for her when she was a girl, but she'd never cope now. If there's any way I can help you fight this, I will. It's abominable."

"She doesn't realise I know, but most of her savings are gone too," Gloria added, standing up shakily, and taking a deep breath. "Right," she announced, "that's enough of my troubles." She blew her nose. "Anyway, it's hardly your fault, Flic. I shouldn't have burdened you. It does do me good to come here, it really does. Look, if we don't open one of those boxes soon, we'll never get your books sorted."

By the time Gloria had to leave, one bookcase had been successfully assembled and was lying on its back on the carpet.

"And we didn't misplace a single screw," Gloria announced with a mixture of pride and astonishment.

She assured Felicity that she would bring a drill with her the next day, so that they could fix it safely to the wall. Although it was Saturday, her mum was living with her now, so she would be able to leave Alice at home. But Felicity had foreseen a slight problem.

"I was planning to take my heavy curtains to the launderette tomorrow before we hang them. I didn't get a chance to clean them when I was packing up in France. Anyway, that means I may be out when you arrive. How about I give you my spare set of keys so you can let yourself in at the main entrance? In fact, you can hang on to them, if that's all right with you?"

"Yeah, that'll be fine. Good idea."

Felicity was relieved to note that Gloria had lost all her inhibitions over coming here.

"Assuming I'm not around, you could make a start on the second bookcase, and I'll help you mount them after lunch. Would that be OK? Oh… and why doesn't

Alice bring her swimming cossie when she comes at half-term? We could go for a swim, as long as you're happy with that."

"She'd absolutely love that pool. But I warn you, you'll never be able to get her out of the water once she's in."

"See you some time tomorrow then." Felicity raised her arms. "Faire les bises?"

Gloria looked puzzled, but when her friend bent in to kiss her on each cheek, she understood.

Felicity
Lily's Launderette, Dunborough, England
October 7th 2017

Felicity set off for the launderette shortly after eight-thirty the next morning. Her laundry bag was heavier than she had expected, so her walk was punctuated with tiny rests along the way, offering her the opportunity to greet people and generally watch the world go by. Not so long ago, she reflected, a visit from the postman and a quick 'bonjour' would have made her day. The streets were busier than usual, and she noticed a large group of tourists congregating around a local guide. Felicity wondered how much of their surroundings these strangers were actually taking in, as they brandished their phones and smiled for 'selfies'. She couldn't bear to think of herself being herded around like these poor souls. Where was their sense of enterprise and adventure? Some of the cafés still had a few tables and chairs outside, so she decided to stop for a quick coffee within sight of the abbey and the museum. As the waitress placed her cup of espresso in front of her,

Felicity smiled to herself. She had taken a group of children to this very museum, oh so many years ago. You counted them in and you counted them out, she recalled. Inevitably the numbers hadn't tallied and it had fallen to Felicity to conduct the search for the missing child. She had found him thoroughly engrossed in a display of ancient weapons inside the main hall and felt reluctant to pull him away. Alas, she realised, such an outing may not even be permitted nowadays, given all the health and safety requirements that modern schools were subject to. Felicity frowned. There's no way she would ever want to become a teacher nowadays, and she felt pleased that neither Alice nor Emily had wanted to follow in her footsteps. Teachers were no longer required to show initiative and as for being led by the children's interests, well that was totally off the cards.

Felicity paid for her coffee and set off on the final stretch to locate the launderette. As she passed the Charter Hotel, the doorman was standing on the pavement about to summon a taxi. He greeted her affably, and Felicity felt stupidly gratified. Turning the corner, she found herself in a maze of slightly more downmarket streets and alleyways. At the far end, in large blue lettering, she spotted the words LILY'S LAUNDERETTE. She drew nearer and saw that the wide glass double frontage was seething with a mass of painted white soap bubbles. They rose from pavement level, frothing and popping on their upward flight. Felicity half expected to see them floating off over the chimney pots into that bright blue patch of sky beyond. Maybe she would even discover the 'Lovely Lily' inside.

"Thank goodness," she muttered to herself as she nudged the glass door open with the front of her laundry bag. "I couldn't have carried this an inch further." Leaving her burden in the middle of the floor, she started to look around. "My God, it hasn't changed a bit," she marvelled.

She had to admit that the machines themselves were a bit more refined nowadays. Large stainless-steel affairs sat side by side along both walls, like rows of one-eyed Cyclopes waiting to devour the clothes. At the far end she noticed some vending and change machines, dispensing hot drinks, chocolate bars, crisps and coins. The moist air smelled of coffee mixed with the floral overtones of cheap detergent.

"Damn," she muttered. "I've forgotten to bring my own." She would never, ever have forgotten to bring washing powder when she had to count the pennies.

The place was deserted, although the first machine in the row was in use, turning the clothes round and around with a swirl of colour and a slop and a suck. Two empty rows of plastic chairs stood back to back in the middle of the premises, so she gratefully took a seat. Felicity really had to get her breath back if she was ever going to get her head around all this. She closed her eyes briefly.

"Can I help you get some change for the machine, madam?"

Felicity jumped. A young boy had appeared in front of her. No more than nine or ten years of age, he reminded her of so many boys that she had once taught, with his snazzy crew cut, fresh face and disproportionately large front teeth. But in spite of his tender age, this child turned out to be a 'godsend'. With his help she obtained change for a tenner from the machine, bought detergent, and set the appropriate wash for her curtains in the largest machine. He told her authoritatively that there was no point hanging around to put them into the dryer, but that she should give him enough coins so that he could do it for her. If she would like to return in two hours, her curtains would be ready for her.

Felicity felt light-hearted as she walked back towards the town, freed of her heavy load. She had decided to pass the time shopping for a gift. It would soon be her youngest daughter's birthday, and she remembered seeing a nice art shop hidden away beside the abbey where she might find something suitable, or if nothing else, a nice card to send. She spent a long time browsing amongst their pictures and artefacts, finally selecting an art calendar for her daughter which she thought she might be tempted to keep for herself. There was still a little time to kill so she returned to that same café for a second espresso. It was only after she had taken her seat that she began to feel misgivings. Should that child have even been there on his own like that? Oh God, and what about all those coins she had given him for the dryer? She fretted that she may not get any back. Would she even see her curtains again for that matter? At her age, Felicity reflected, one was inclined to make silly mistakes. One of the angels seemed to be leaning away from her Heavenly climb to cast her a baleful look, as if in tacit agreement.

On returning to the launderette, she was not wholly surprised, but certainly disconcerted, to see that the premises were deserted, and the kid was nowhere to be seen. She spun around in a panic, searching wildly for her curtains. All the dryers were empty, while one solitary wash slopped backwards and forwards in the corner. Even her laundry bag had vanished. She slumped down onto a chair, hoping to calm her heart that was now turning somersaults inside her frail body. What a fool to have been taken in like that.

Just then, a door opened in the opposite wall. Felicity looked up to see an older man of about sixty years of age standing in the door frame. There was a large comfortable armchair behind him, and a desk with papers strewn all over it.

"Ah, thank goodness there's someone around here. Are you in charge? I think… I think I've just been robbed."

The man didn't react. He just looked steadily at Felicity and shook his head sadly. "It's all right, Miss Jones. No need to panic. That would have been Fred, my grandson. He likes to help me around here."

"But… how… who…?"

"Can I get you a cup of tea, Miss? If you just stay sitting there, I'll go and put the kettle on in my office. I don't really like tea from those machines, do you? Awful stuff… tastes of dishwater."

Felicity slumped back down onto the plastic seat, continuing to scan the premises for her curtains as the kettle came to the boil. She searched inside the dryers and under every seat; she surveyed the machine tops, and investigated the corner by the door, but all to no avail.

"Here you are, Miss Jones. You look a bit shocked, so I've put extra sugar in it."

"Oh… er… thank you Mr…?"

"Just call me Albert. Your curtains are safe with me in the office. Fred likes to help our customers out, just like I did when I was a lad. Except it was Mr Stewart who owned this place of course back then, when you and me used to do our washing here."

"But…?"

"He didn't use all of your coins, as them curtains were quite quick to dry. But if you like, I can keep one back for him as a tip. It's up to you, mind."

Felicity was more than happy to agree, and Albert counted the remaining pound coins into her trembling hands.

"Drink up, Miss. I don't like to see you like this. You were always so kind to us."

"Albert? I think I might remember you. Didn't you…?"

"Of course, Miss. You was a teacher back then at Sunnyvale. I never forget a face. You came to our house the day our mum went to the hospital. Me and Lillian seen you when we was all doin' our washin' together here, so's we invited you round for a cup of tea. When we told our mum afterwards, she was really proud."

Felicity took a few sips. The tea tasted surprisingly good, even though she normally couldn't abide sugar. She began to appraise this considerate man who was still bending over her in concern.

"I was so sorry, Albert, when I heard that your mum had died. Mrs Cherry told me about it after I had left. It must have been hard for you."

"It was, Miss Jones. But they kept Lillian and me together at The Children's Home. Then when my dad could cope, we all got together again. They gave us one of those nice new build council houses too."

"And the baby?"

"He was with foster parents at first. But he's not a baby no more, Miss. He'll be fifty this year. Lives in Australia."

"And what about Lillian? Where is she now?" Felicity was frantically trying to work things out. After all, the sign at the front did call this Lily's Launderette. "Does she own…?"

Albert shook his head gravely. "She died, Miss, last year. Cancer… like our mum. But I didn't like to change the name. That's what everybody knows us by… Lily's."

"But how? I mean… who exactly does the launderette belong to?"

"It belongs to me, and after I've gone it'll go to my son. He's good on computers. That's his full-time job, but he helps me here with all the administration and stuff like that."

"But how…?"

"You mean how come I own the place? That's all down to Mr Stewart really. He owned the business back then, when we all used to come here. Then, after me and Lillian moved back, I used to hang around a bit, helping customers for the odd tip. I got to know all those machines; how to unblock them, and things like that. Then, at the end of every day I'd help Mr Stewart wash the floors and everything. When I left school, he said he was getting a bit old to be doing everything himself, so he'd like to take me on. I've never worked anywhere else. When he died, he didn't have no children, so he left the business to me."

Felicity felt a swell of pride on behalf of this good man. But poor Lillian. She was such a sweet child, always eager to please. Felicity had long harboured the opinion that many of the children at Sunnyvale had been selected for other than educational reasons. For how could Albert with his business acumen and social skills ever have been considered 'subnormal'. Good old Albert!

"I kept the curtains in the office, Miss, thinking you might want me to help you fold them. It'll make ironing much easier for you. But they're very heavy. Are you up for it?"

Felicity carried her empty cup back into Albert's office, and soon they were standing at either end of the launderette folding the long green and mauve drapes between them. Albert commanded operations, and within minutes her patio curtains had been folded up neatly and packed inside her laundry bag. At that moment the door of the launderette opened and a smartly dressed older woman walked in holding a laundry bag in one hand, while a little girl of around six or seven hung on to the other. Felicity couldn't help but smile at the child's delightful hairstyle; her cheerful brown face framed by a multitude of tight plaits, each one carefully woven with colourful beads. As for her probable grandmother, she made Felicity feel exceedingly scruffy in her worn jeans and leather boots. Could this be Gloria's mum, she wondered? The little girl seemed to be around the right age, so that would fit, and Gloria had certainly been right about there being few black faces in Dunborough. Felicity was thinking rapidly now. It would be good to meet, but this was neither the right place, nor the right time. Picking up her laundry bag, she prepared to make a quick departure.

"Well, it was great catching up with you, Albert. And please say thank you to that grandson of yours for all his help."

As Felicity nudged open the door with her laundry bag, she stole a glance at the other woman. The little girl was tugging at the sleeve of her tailored jacket, while she stared fixedly in the opposite direction.

"Nana, Nana, please can we go to the park after we've put the washing in? Albert always says he'll put it in the dryer for us. Please, please... can we?"

At that point, Felicity slipped outside.

Tina
Grove Park, Dunborough, England
October 7th 2017

"You're not to go on the big slide. Stick to that one over there. It's much safer for you."

"Aw, Nana, I'm nearly seven. Winston lets me."

"Well, I'm not going to. There's lots of other things you can play on."

But Alice was already out of earshot, dashing to join the other kids in the children's area of the local park. Tina watched as her granddaughter jumped onto a swing and began to rock herself backwards and forwards in an ever increasing arc. She'd spent time this morning doing her hair in cornrows. Alice looked so pretty with those colourful beads swinging out on the ends of her braids. She surely was the sweetest little girl ever born. Tina remembered how she had longed to see this sight again as she tossed and turned night after night under the unremitting light of her detention centre room. And here she was. She had cried so much in recent days, but the tears that escaped her now were tears of joy. They would go to the pond later to feed the ducks. This was something that Gloria had liked doing when she was small, and Tina had saved some bread from breakfast. She would have to do something about contributing to the food bill, though, now that they were living together, but quite how, she wasn't sure. Paying rent and bills for six months out of her savings had pretty well stripped her of cash. How could she possibly have fallen so low, when she was soaring so high? If this was what could happen to you in this country, why did she even bother getting all those qualifications?

"Nana, Nana."

Tina looked up to see Alice in front of her, standing hand in hand with another child: a little white girl with shoulder-length chestnut coloured hair and a gappy grin.

"This is Amy. She's my best friend at school." They hugged each other as if to confirm this, and then rushed off laughing back to the swings.

Tina watched them happily playing there, reflecting that when she had first arrived here at the age of ten, she had no friends whatsoever. How delighted she was for Alice. Of course, it hadn't helped Tina that she had been promptly sent to another school on the edge of town, picked up every day in a special taxi. Did they really believe that she was stupid? Well, they had got that wrong, hadn't they? A harsh voice intruded into her reverie.

"Amy, Amy, come here when I tell you."

"Aw, Dad."

Tina watched the small child reluctantly jump from the swing that Alice was pushing, and trail towards the perimeter fence.

"We've got to go home now."

"But Dad. You said we could stay here all morning. Why do we have to go home now?"

"Because I'm saying so, that's why."

"Can't I just go and say goodbye to Alice?"

"No. I'm telling you to come NOW."

Tina felt sickened and resisted an urge to rush over to Alice. If only she could wrap her up in gossamer and protect her feelings for ever and ever. But she knew that she couldn't, so she just sat tight, waiting for her granddaughter to return. Alice would have to learn to receive such knocks, just as Gloria had. As for that daughter of hers, goodness knows why she'd gone to help some stuck up white woman move house. Not just any old house either, but one of those grand apartments by the river. She could get a perfectly good job if she tried. Tina heard a cry and looked up. There was Alice coming back to her at last.

"Can we go and feed the ducks now, Nana?

"Sure, honey. Good job I didn't finish all my toast this morning, eh?"

Their path led them through an area of wide flower beds, flanked by a variety of exotic shrubs and trees. This was a place that Tina liked to visit often, especially in spring when she would come to see the daffodils and those huge drifts of cherry blossom, albeit a few months apart.

"Look, baby doll. The trees are turning for autumn. Aren't the colours beautiful?"

But Alice barely noticed in her desperation to see the ducks. "Nana, Nana, there they are over by the little island." Alice started bouncing up and down in her excitement. Within seconds her voice was drowned out by a cacophony of quacking mallards, each one greedily trying to be at the head of the queue.

Tina sat down on a nearby bench and began to reflect. She prayed desperately that Alice would never lose her joyful optimism; she sure was a delightful kid. But one thing was certain, she was always going to receive some knocks. It had been hard for Tina and for Gloria. It was going to be hard for Alice, too. Perhaps she would be better going to school in Bristol where she wouldn't stick out like a sore thumb. As for Winston, she felt proud of him, such a lovely considerate lad. But then so was Stephen Lawrence. She spotted some delicate mauve autumn crocuses at the edge of the path, peeping out from the undergrowth like an old friend. When her own mum came here with Gloria, she had said how much she missed seeing jacarandas and banana palms. But Jamaica just felt like some distant island covered in mist to Tina. She could barely remember anything about it. She had grown familiar with the yearly succession of less dramatic blooms. For Tina, daffodils and bluebells in spring, and walking through the dripping park on a miserable day, were signs of home.

Felicity
Avon Court, Dunborough, England
October 20th 2017

Felicity bumped into Joan at the head of the stairs. She was conversing intently with a casually dressed man in his sixties whom Felicity had seen about the corridors from time to time, and another slightly older man in tweeds who looked the epitome of a Tory toff. As she approached, they quickly attenuated their conversation.

"Ah hello, Felicity, let me introduce you to Mr Williams and Dr Cherry from Flats 4 and 6. We're on the Residents' Committee together."

Dr Cherry held his hand out to her. "John, it's nice to finally meet you, Felicity."

"Nice to meet you too."

Somewhat more reluctantly, Mr Williams did the same, introducing himself as Robert.

Turning towards Joan, Felicity asked, "Any news concerning my joining you yet?"

She detected a sudden confusion as Joan and Robert began speaking at the same time. John seemed to withdraw himself slightly from the group. But… surely, she must have been mistaken. Did he really just give her a sly wink?

"Ah no, er well…" Robert stuttered.

"It usually takes a bit of time before one hears, dear," Joan was explaining. "Usual formalities you know."

Felicity wasn't really bothered one way or another but couldn't help noticing a furtive look between the two as she picked up her shopping and left them to it. Shortly afterwards, she heard a tap at her door. Of course, it was Joan.

"Hello again, or 'Rebonjour' as they say in France," Felicity joked. "I'm just having some tea. Would you like a cup? Milk? Two sugars?"

"That would be very kind, thank you. I thought I'd pop along and have a quiet word," Joan confided. "Just between the two of us."

Felicity had placed her shopping bag on top of the counter and was now filling the kettle. She hadn't a clue what was coming but decided to make the tea first as Joan was barely audible from the kitchen. As she busied herself with tea leaves and mugs, she had the opportunity to watch her neighbour taking in every detail of her newly furnished apartment. She had just accepted delivery of the white leather sofa on which Joan was now gracefully reposing. She seemed much more interested in studying the new furnishings than enjoying the wonderful river view, and she swivelled her eyes round from time to time to take in the bookshelves, the new dining table, chairs and coffee table which had all been craftsman built from lovely light oak. She then proceeded to appraise Felicity's favourite Murano lamp. Alistair had chosen it on that last trip to Venice, and Felicity had just unearthed it from the bottom of the very last packing case. It looked impressive standing on the low table.

"Ahem," Joan coughed delicately, after she had taken her first tentative sip of tea.

"Earl Grey," Felicity informed her. "I hope you like it."

"Oh yes, lovely dear," Joan agreed. "Ahem," she coughed again. "It's just that the Residents' Committee aren't entirely happy about one or two matters. They feel that we should clear the air, so to speak, before you join us."

"Yes?"

"Oh dear, I hope this isn't going to offend you."

Felicity felt sure that whatever was coming was certainly going to offend her, so perhaps she was a little unkind to be enjoying Joan's obvious discomfort.

"It's just that... that... they aren't happy about your cleaner woman coming in whenever she likes. She seems to have her own key."

"Yes. She does."

"Well... isn't that... you know?"

"What?"

"Er... er... risky."

"Risky?" Felicity couldn't help but laugh.

"Yes, dear. Not everyone is to be trusted you know."

Felicity could not believe what she was hearing. She steadied her voice and tried to remain cool. "Joan, it's quite safe for Gloria to have a key. In fact, I would be offended if anyone said otherwise. She's a friend."

"Oh." Joan eased herself slowly from the settee and turned towards the door. "I just thought I should tell you what some of the others were saying, dear. Of course, it doesn't bother me one bit." As she got to the door she turned and added, "Oh yes, and certain members wanted me to mention the swimming pool. You took a child in there the other day... twice."

"Yes. Last Tuesday. Why? Are they concerned? I am entitled to invite guests, aren't I?"

"It's just that the child was... er... er... you know."

Felicity did know only too well, but when Joan saw the appalled look on her face, she quickly changed tack.

"What I mean to say is that the committee think that the swimming pool should be reserved for adults. Children do tend to make a lot of noise don't they, dear?"

"And if my grandson comes to visit from the States, should I not be able to take him?"

"Ah well, I am sure the committee would make an exception in that case. Oh dear, I nearly forgot. I've left something cooking on my stove."

Felicity waited until Joan had headed off, leaving the door behind her slightly ajar. She pushed it open further and peered down the corridor to see her neighbour retreating towards the stairwell. Then she turned towards her latest friend, Alexa.

"Play Edith Piaf please, Alexa. Loud!"

Alexa obeyed, and the strains of 'Je ne regrette rien' filled the corridors, ably abetted by Felicity herself.

Later, when she went to retrieve her neighbour's cup, she noticed that the tea had barely been touched.

Felicity
The Minstrel Inn, Dunborough, England
October 21st 2017

Gloria had found a new job. When she had called Felicity the previous evening to tell her, they had agreed to meet the next day for a pub lunch to settle a few things. Felicity suddenly realised that they had never discussed a rate of pay for Gloria's help and, now that she wanted to settle up, she didn't quite know what to do. In truth she felt the discussion of monetary matters to be rather distasteful. She wanted to be generous, for Gloria's help had been invaluable. However, she didn't want to appear like 'Lady Bountiful', as that would be too demeaning for Gloria. In the event, Gloria took the matter into her own hands.

"I've made a list of the days and the hours I worked," she said as she was edging her way along the leather banquette, and she immediately slipped a piece of paper onto the table between them.

Feeling embarrassed, Felicity quickly noted the total number of hours worked and took a relieved breath.

"I used to earn £9.50 an hour at the Charter," Gloria continued. "Do you think that would be fair?"

"Oh, more than fair. I think you deserve a bit more, considering all that creative flair you brought with you. What would you say to £12.50? Is that about right do you think?"

Gloria was delighted to accept, and so the awkward subject of remuneration was quickly dismissed.

"By the way, lunch is on me. Now what are we going to drink to celebrate your new job?"

"I'd better not have too much," Gloria warned, as Felicity returned to the table a couple of minutes later carrying two glasses of rosé.

They raised their glasses and clinked.

"Cheers! Here's to your new job. Now you must tell me all about it."

"Well, Flic, it's all down to you in a way. I'm ever so excited. Have you seen that art shop round the corner from the abbey?"

Felicity certainly had.

"Well, it's there. They were looking for a new sales assistant. I didn't hardly dare apply. But then we've been talking about art so much recently, and you've taught me such a lot, I thought why the hell don't I try for it? I really got on well with the owner and she offered me the job. I still can't believe it."

"Congratulations." Felicity raised her glass once more.

"They sell a lot of reproductions and posters and

stuff, mainly to tourists. But they've also got some original work by local artists and art materials too. I'm surprised she didn't just think I talked a lot of rubbish."

"Gloria, you underestimate yourself. You deserve this job. You really do. Actually, I was in there the other day. I shall miss you though. Do you mind if I come in and buy something from time to time?"

"Oh no… I mean no, you won't miss me. If you want me to, I'll still clean for you. How about I come on Sunday mornings?"

Felicity was only too delighted to agree. "Well, that's settled. You may as well keep the keys I gave you. In fact, if you want to start a week tomorrow, that's fine by me, but I'm afraid I won't be there. My youngest daughter Emily has actually invited me to stay with her over that weekend, and I'll be going up by train. It's her birthday."

They paused while the waitress set up the table for food and took their orders, allowing Felicity to survey their surroundings. She noticed one or two people quickly turn away when she looked up, as if they had been the subject of curiosity. She also noticed a log fire blazing in the open grate, in spite of the mild autumn weather. In her mind that was the mark of a good English pub. If there was one thing she had missed above all while living in France, it was the chance to have a cosy drink within warming range of an English pub fire.

"Do you know I never asked how your meeting with

the lawyer went," she added.

"Oh, it's hard to say."

Someone on a nearby table began laughing hysterically, causing the ambient noise to rise by a few decibels as people struggled to make themselves heard above it. Felicity pulled her chair closer to the table. What she would have given at that moment to be back in France, where the serious business of eating was carried out in near silence, and only after the dessert and a full complement of wine would you ever hear laughter or even slightly raised voices. Ah well, she thought, one can't have everything.

"He works for free on behalf of the Refugee Council," Gloria continued raising her voice. "He really couldn't have been more sympathetic with my mum. He's discussing what to do next with our MP. But what he did say for certain is that this should never ever have happened. The Home Office have got things completely wrong."

"So, your mum doesn't have to worry anymore?"

"Well…" Gloria pulled a face. "It's not going to be quite that easy. She still feels under threat of deportation. The Home Office seem to want to do their own thing, whatever our MP is saying. You know, Flic, what they did to her was horrible, and nobody has ever even thought to apologise. That's how much concern they have for her."

"But now you know about it, you can fight tooth and nail to make sure it doesn't happen again."

"Sure. There's a lot of people gunning for her now. If they try and take her away again, it'll be over my dead body." Gloria took an angry gulp of wine. "Every night I've got to listen to my mum crying herself to sleep, and she's lost so much weight... it's horrible. Alice isn't herself either. I'm sure this is upsetting her. You know, Flic, Mum used to be the strength of our family, but now..."

The waitress arrived bearing two plates, so they each moved their drinks aside to receive them. "One pasta alla vongole," she announced with a beaming smile, "and one spaghetti carbonara. Enjoy!"

For a moment neither felt like eating. Felicity wondered what sort of toad could do this to a fellow human being... all thanks to Theresa May and her 'hostile environment'. To think that Britain, the country of her birth, could treat people in such an abominable fashion. Sometimes she felt like shouting 'not in my name!' to the heavens. But that was just stupid. As a British citizen this, and many other atrocious deeds, had been carried out in her name, whether she liked it or not.

"Look," she said eventually, "we'd better eat before it gets cold. Bon appétit."

They clinked glasses again.

"Here's to your mum."

Felicity took a forkful of pasta alla vongole. She had to admit that British pub food had improved immensely since she had left, and she couldn't help thinking that France was living on its past reputation.

"By the way," she added, "I think I might have seen your mum in the launderette with Alice the other Saturday. She didn't say anything?"

"No… I don't think so."

"She went to school in Dunborough, you said?"

"Hmm." Gloria frowned. "That's another awful thing. She didn't go to the ordinary secondary school like I did. Just after she'd arrived here to live with my nana, they sent her to a school for the 'educationally subnormal'. Subnormal? If my wonderful mother is subnormal, then this government, the whole education authority, and every teacher that has ever existed are bleedin' cretins."

*

As Felicity bade farewell to Gloria in front of the abbey, she paused for a second to watch the struggling stone angels, her kindred souls, still striving to reach Heaven. She liked to think of the stonemasons having their little bit of fun and vowed to go searching for gargoyles one of these days. But it was such a pleasant afternoon that she thought she would take a stroll towards the park. She was feeling slightly uneasy and wished to clear her head. For some reason her arthritis was playing her up today. She was walking stiffly, and her back and shoulders ached.

Felicity's pace was slow as she climbed the hill, but it picked up a bit as she entered the sweep of the

Georgian crescent where she had once lived. She had been back in Dunborough for weeks, and yet she hadn't even thought to revisit her very first flat. She noticed that someone had placed some plants on the steps leading down to the basement patio, but their leaves were beginning to wither. As if in defiance, a single scarlet geranium continued to flourish. Felicity hoped that whoever lived there now had felt the same magic as she had. She admired the expensive looking drapes at the window and longed to peer further inside. Of course, when it had been her home, heavy curtains were beyond her reach. Tourists would swing against the iron railings above her flat and gaze quizzically at her sparse furnishings. At night there were ancient wooden shutters to obscure their view, and she liked to imagine how the servants of old would close those very shutters when their work was done.

Her step picked up further as she negotiated the cobbles and rounded the crescent before entering the park. The air was clearer here, and the noise of traffic had abated, so she raised her head and took a deep breath. The overhead trees were stirring in the gentle breeze, and she watched a yellow sycamore leaf, taken by a sudden gust of air, spiral languidly towards the ground. She had spent two autumns of her life in this place and was excited to return. Children were calling happily from the playpark ahead, and she recalled the many different schools and playgrounds that she had known. How she missed those happy sounds nowadays;

that freedom and innocence that only children know.

It was still quite early, so she decided to walk to the end of the park and continue from there towards her old school. As she skirted the pond, she noticed Alice standing at the water's edge, tugging excitedly at the jacket of a tall young man.

"That must be Winston," she thought.

She had so much enjoyed looking after her, and would have loved to greet her, but she continued on her way, anxious not to intrude. But something made her stop and glance back. There was her grandmother, standing in the shade of a tall shrub. Neither greeted each other, but Felicity felt certain that a bond had been acknowledged.

Her pace picked up further. It felt as though her arthritis had never even existed as her limbs loosened and her energy returned. She was following a minor tree-lined road now, and the further she walked the larger and further apart the houses became. It was hard to believe that anybody lived in this neighbourhood. All she could hear was the muffled sound of a car in the distance and a thrush singing from a branch above her head. At last she reached her destination, 'Greenfields Academy, Private School for children aged three to thirteen'. The large school gates were closed. After all, it was Saturday, and there would be little or no traffic. She investigated a small pedestrian access to the side and, after a quick glance around, she slipped through. How well she knew this road that led from the gate to the small stately mansion at the top of the drive. Keeping close to the verge, she ventured on until she was standing on the gravel forecourt in front of the main entrance. Above her loomed that familiar building, barely changed from all those years ago. Of course, the double doors appeared to be firmly locked, but she could picture the inner hall which lay behind them, with its polished parquet floor, the headmistress's office to the side, and the wide sweep of stairs that led to her classroom. Looking up, she recognised the stone-clad oriel window on the first floor where she sometimes stood looking out at the surrounding park. But without children, this was a mere building, not a school. Everything was eerily quiet. Even the wind had dropped.

Felicity suddenly felt uneasy and turned away, only too aware that she was trespassing. But what the hell? She had come this far, hadn't she? Skirting the house, she passed the sixties built domestic science block, and the red brick dining hall where she and her pupils had feasted on endless plates of stew, mashed potato, custard and steamed puddings. From there she took the smaller path that led to the top field. This was where the children were free to play on fine days. Feeling much more sprightly than she might have expected, Felicity wandered around getting her bearings.

"You all right, Miss?"

"Ah Simon," she exclaimed, greeting with enormous pleasure the little boy who had appeared from behind a bush. She tousled his familiar crop of golden hair and reached for a tissue to wipe the slight dribble that covered his chin. But then she remembered that Simon, bless him, always had a dribble. "Yes, I'm fine, Simon, thank you. How are you?"

"M-M-Miss? You all right, Miss?" he repeated, then just as suddenly as he had appeared, he vanished into the bushes. There were so many bushes and trees around here, a child could easily go missing, but when the bell went, they always turned up.

Goodness, there was Sharon. Such a beautiful child. Her mum always took such great care to dress her long hair in ribbons. Today her ribbons were scarlet, and her auburn hair shone in the afternoon sun. But Sharon didn't greet Felicity. She ran past her, ploughing her lonely furrow backwards and forwards, up and down the length of the field, shaking her head from side to side and smiling, as if in private conversation with herself. Sharon lived in an enchanted world that Felicity was not permitted to enter.

"What time is it, Miss?"

Goodness, it was William. Felicity had forgotten all about William, but there he was, tugging at her elbow in his short grey trousers, blue cotton shirt and very smart tie.

"Hello, William. My goodness you do look smart today, and how nice it is to see you. It's three o'clock, William."

Her pupil looked worried. He reached out and slipped

his hand into hers. "What time is it, Miss?" he fretted.

Felicity tousled his hair in response and turned away to find somewhere to sit. There was a very large tree stump sticking out of the ground so she decided to place her puffa jacket on the grass and rest against its rough bark for a while. William joined her and sat alongside, worming his stubby little fingers between hers once more. She remembered the magnificent redwood that would once have towered above them in this very spot. Sadly, it had to be felled, in spite of objections from neighbouring houses, as it was suffering from a progressive disease and put the children at risk. It still functioned as an excellent back rest, however, and for a brief moment Felicity closed her eyes. The breeze was picking up again and, deprived of her coat, she felt a slight chill. Surely William, with his bare muddy knees and short grey trousers, must be feeling chilly too? She reached to draw him close, but he was no longer there.

Suddenly, a jay screeched its way between two oak trees as it gathered acorns to store against the winter ahead. It would seem now that everyone had vanished, save for a small group of teenage girls who were huddling together under a giant beech tree. She recognised her own group of older girls, the ones she took for drama and English lessons most afternoons. They saw themselves as different from the other pupils, and Felicity could sympathise with their frustrations. Of course, they didn't want anything to do with her. They turned away, clearly plotting something. There was

Denise, so worldly wise that she made Felicity feel utterly naïve, with her skirt hoisted beneath her belt miniskirt style and a faint hint of nicotine pervading the air around her. Denise was the leader of the gang. Martha, bless her cotton socks, looked up to Denise, but she had little to say, and Anne tried to hold her own, but was generally overridden. The fourth member of the group, who was standing slightly apart from the rest, was Tina. Tina was an important member of the group, but she generally kept her own counsel. She looked at Felicity from underneath her brow and turned away.

"Oi. What ya doin' 'ere, Grandma? Don't you know this place is private?"

"Oh, I'm so sorry. I didn't mean to…"

"Ga'arn… scarper before I call the police."

Felicity was looking up into the large square unshaven face of a middle-aged man. He wasn't a pretty sight. She noticed a Group 4 logo sewn onto his jacket.

"It's… it's just that I used to teach here you see," she ventured.

"You deaf or summat? Get yer arse owt of 'ere. And be quick about it."

Felicity was flabbergasted. Why on earth did schools need to be policed by ill-mannered thuggish security guards nowadays? Where was Mr Brown, that dear old fashioned school caretaker in his brown cotton overall, who always had a pail of sawdust handy, and carried the crates of milk into the classrooms for the pupils? Now, he was a real gentleman. No matter how busy he was, he would always ask after her every day when she arrived at school. As Felicity struggled to raise herself from the ground, she fretted about what her country was coming to, treating everyone like potential criminals. But her limbs now felt as soft as play doh, and she couldn't get any purchase, so she turned to get a grip on a protruding dead branch.

"I'm… I'm so sorry," she apologised, as she fell over her feet. "Can't you see I wasn't doing any harm?"

But he didn't want to know. As he raised a walkie talkie to his mouth, she really began to panic. Her new-found agility had suddenly deserted her, and she felt old and diminished, while all this time the onlooker just leered and threatened.

Felicity couldn't remember how she got back to her apartment. She must have walked all the way, as it was almost dark when she got there, and the lights from her building were spinning and dancing on the rippled surface of the river before it churned over the weir. As soon as Felicity opened the door of her apartment, she collapsed onto the sofa and fell asleep. But she had been followed.

"Can we go for a walk, Miss?"

"Yes, Miss. I hates doing English. Why don't you take us to see the horses."

"Miss, Miss, pleeese!"

How come those girls had turned up at her home? They seemed to want nothing to do with her earlier. But the idea of a walk was certainly appealing. They had visited the horses together before, and once they were outside the classroom her group had always relaxed and talked more freely. Even Felicity had enjoyed it and felt complicit in their escape. What was English teaching about, after all, if it wasn't to help her pupils express themselves, rather than sitting in some stuffy classroom, filling the correct word in a meaningless sentence that they would most probably never use or even understand?

"Oh, all right then girls. Come on. Have we got anything to feed them with?"

"I saved an apple from dinner time, Miss," Anne volunteered.

Felicity couldn't help giggling with the rest. It had all been a carefully contrived plot. They picked up the footpath from the school field that led downhill towards the boundary fence. Beyond lay a small, fenced paddock which belonged to a neighbouring property. The girls had named the ponies that grazed there Tonto and Star. Rarely had Felicity seen them look so interested or content, as they stroked the ponies' muzzles and reached out to rub behind their ears.

"Ouch, he bit me," Anne wailed.

Felicity took her hand and showed her how to bend her thumb back when offering a piece of apple.

"Give us a piece," Denise demanded of her timid friend. "Let's have a go." She had shed her knowing 'grown up' persona and was now as excited as a small child. Even Denise, with all her worldly ways, was needy and vulnerable.

Felicity sometimes wondered whether this sheltered, semi-rural environment was maybe good for them after all. But then it seemed so wrong that they were cut off from their neighbourhood friends. To keep these lively girls here until they reached school leaving age seemed cruel and misguided. How would they ever cope in the real world? Felicity feared that they were destined to be outsiders for the rest of their lives.

"Right, back to the classroom, girls," she suddenly announced. "You'd better all finish those sentences in your book so we can show Mrs Harris what you have been doing this afternoon." This was slightly dishonest, as she knew the headmistress felt exactly as she did and liked to see her taking a fresh approach. But many of her colleagues did not. Felicity sensed that some even resented her for introducing a little dissension into the staffroom.

"Aw, do we have to, Miss?" Tina grumbled. "Blackboard sentences are a waste of time." Tina had continued to hang back from the rest of the group, but even she dropped her guard and grew excited when a pony tried to nuzzle its head in the crook of her shoulder.

"Miss, have you got a boyfriend, Miss?"

My God, what was Denise saying? Felicity realised that she had better put a stop to this inappropriate conversation right away.

"Are you on the pill, Miss?" Denise persisted. "I am, Miss. It's really easy. You just have to go and ask your doctor."

Anne was nodding wisely in agreement, while Felicity noticed that Martha looked completely baffled. It was Tina's reaction that worried her most. She had picked up on Felicity's embarrassment and now, as they started to climb back up towards the school, she was encouraging her friend to stir the pot. By the time they entered her classroom, the two girls were laughing hysterically and cavorting around.

"Stop it at once," Felicity shouted. "Get to your desks and open your jotters. I'm going to put some sentences on the board. I want you to copy them out and put the right word in the box. If you haven't finished by the time the bell goes, there'll be trouble. I'll be coming round to help you when I'm finished."

Denise flounced to her desk, but then sat down meekly. Poor Anne and Martha looked rather afraid. Tina, however, was not prepared to accept this sudden change in the proceedings. She sat down with a provocative look, and slowly started to raise her desk lid, inch by inch. Felicity could hear her muttering behind it. She obviously said something to Denise because both of them hooted so loudly that Felicity feared that it must have reverberated throughout the building.

"Stop… it… at… once," Felicity repeated at the very top of her voice. "Tina, if you don't get your jotter out

NOW, you will be going to Mrs Harris' office."

Tina was silent for a second. Then she shut her desk lid with a reverberating slam and stood up. "You wouldn't dare," she challenged. "What about Denise? She was laughing too. You're only getting at me because I'm black."

When Felicity woke, the room was in complete darkness, save for a few scattered lights that were reflected from the weir. She adjusted a sofa cushion under her head and continued lying there, deep in reflection. What had she done with that poem? The one that Tina had subsequently written in her jotter? It had been a brilliant and moving cry for help, offered to her teacher in apology for her outburst. And Felicity hadn't done a thing about it.

Felicity
Avon Court, Dunborough, England
November 3rd 2017

Her train was almost deserted as it pulled into
Dunborough Station, so Felicity waited until the doors
had opened before quickly picking up her case and
descending onto the platform. The overheated carriage
had made her feel sleepy, but now a chill wind was
blowing down the platform and stirring her into action.
It had been nice spending time with Emily and her
partner. Now that her daughter's life was more settled,
she had seemed kinder somehow and more welcoming,
even inviting her to stay on longer than originally
intended. Felicity zipped her puffa coat up to her neck,
pulled on her leather gloves, and set off, wheeling her
small case behind her.

This was the first time that she had left Dunborough
since her arrival over six weeks ago, and it felt good to
be returning. The lights were coming on early in the
shops, dispelling all thoughts of the approaching winter.
She would stop off at the supermarket in the centre of

town to buy some groceries and cook herself a fresh pasta dish when she got home. A bottle of Barolo to accompany it might be a good idea, or some other Italian red. The weir mumbled and rumbled away behind her. She reached her apartment building with her purchases and slotted her key in the lock. Somewhere in the distance, a firecracker exploded. At this moment, Felicity felt exceedingly pleased with herself.

"Ah. You're back." Joan was standing facing her in the spacious entrance hall. It was almost as if she had been expecting her.

"Oh hello, Joan. My, it's good to be home. I can't tell you how chilly it is outdoors."

Joan gave her a nervous look, glancing down at her hands, which she was twisting anxiously in front of her.

"Is anything the matter?" asked Felicity. "There's nothing wrong is there?"

"Well… yes… I am afraid to say that actually there is. The Residents' Committee have convened a meeting for later this evening in Mr Williams' place, Flat 4. They would like you to be there."

"Oh good, does that mean I am now a fully accepted member?"

Joan failed to answer. "The meeting is at seven o'clock."

Seven o'clock was such an inconvenient time. But then Felicity remembered the English habit of eating earlier in the evening, and realised that she was going to have to readjust if she wanted to fit in. A welcome gust of warm air greeted her as she opened the door to her apartment. She had stupidly forgotten to adjust the heating while she was away. Alexa did her bit, dutifully switching on all the kitchen spotlights, reflectors and table lamps to bring the flat back to life. Felicity stood still for a moment, her case abandoned by her feet. She looked around slowly as she reacquainted herself with her new apartment. Then she smiled with satisfaction. She had to admit it, with Gloria's help she had created an exceedingly stylish home. Everything was spotless and neatly arranged, save for a piece of torn paper which was lying on the kitchen bench. She picked it up and started to read it out aloud:

"Couldn't come till later, so only did two hours on Sunday. Managed to do the bathroom, kitchen and vacuuming. Hope that's OK. Also stripped the spare bed and put everything in the wash. Didn't have time to iron it, so I've taken it home. Will bring it back next Sunday. See you then, Gloria."

Goodness, Sunday was almost upon them. What could she possibly ask her to do? The flat was spotless. Maybe she would consult Gloria about painting the end wall in a stronger colour. It would be good to have a second opinion, and they could go to B&Q to get what they needed. Felicity decided to prepare a puttanesca sauce before she attended the residents' meeting. She could cook some dried pasta quickly when she returned. But at fifteen minutes to seven she woke up with a start. The mellifluous voice of Barbara was playing on a loop,

126

and for a brief moment she felt nostalgic for her old home in France. She had enough to do without attending this bloomin' meeting and felt rather peeved.

Felicity was slightly late by the time she arrived at Flat 4. Everyone seemed to have been waiting impatiently for her to arrive. She counted five residents excluding herself, all of them formally dressed and pretty elderly. It was hard to guess which one of them could possibly be the renowned 'Colonel' who seemed to reign from above. Everyone there looked pretty innocuous. Joan and Robert were sitting on upright dining chairs. The sofa was occupied by John, and a second gentleman called Peter, of around seventy or seventy-five years of age, whom she had passed once on the stairs. The last member of the group was sitting in an electric wheelchair with his back to the door. Was he, perhaps 'the Colonel'?

"This is Felicity, everyone. As you all know, she recently joined us and is living in Flat 8."

Felicity shuffled her feet awkwardly. It seemed unusually discourteous of Joan not to offer her a seat. John seemed to be patting the cushion that lay vacant in the middle of the sofa so, apologising deferentially, she slipped herself between the two men. He whispered something to her and lightly touched her arm, but God knows what it was he said, because she was feeling quite overwhelmed. Robert coughed and began the proceedings.

"Welcome, everybody. And welcome to our new

fellow resident, Felicity."

"Hear, hear," John called.

Everyone else remained silent.

"In the absence of our chairman, George Evans, I will try and fill everyone in on the distressing events of this week. I'm afraid George sent his apologies but plans to chair our weekly Monday meeting as usual. We have asked Felicity to join us tonight, as we feel these matters will be of concern to her."

"I am surprised the Colonel isn't here, seeing as he discovered the theft," Peter commented rather peevishly.

"Quite," said John.

Felicity felt a frisson of anxiety when she heard the word 'theft', but as the new kid on the block, she knew it would be better to keep a low profile. She rapidly gathered that a member of the Saturday cleaning staff had been asked to dust their prize Picasso bowl, and must have forgotten to lock the display cabinet afterwards. Apparently, the Colonel had discovered that their valued artwork was missing the next day. He had descended in the lift to collect *The Sunday Times* from his postbox and have a lunch time drink at the bar, when he couldn't 'help but notice' that it was no longer there. Felicity was heartbroken. In some strange way, that bowl had formed a connection between her new apartment and her home in France. Who on earth could have stolen it? Everyone was talking in twos or threes as she tried to gather her thoughts. And then she heard these words rise from the hubbub.

"Of course, we all know that Felicity's cleaner has a key."

John pressed his hand firmly on her forearm, as if to restrain her. Felicity froze.

"Keep calm," he whispered.

Felicity couldn't think straight. All she knew was that people were talking about Gloria with hostility and suspicion, and she was too confused to defend her. It made her feel utterly disloyal.

"Don't worry," John continued in a low voice. "Call into my flat on the way back, and we'll talk this over."

The hubbub continued.

"I want to know why we haven't called the police already," said the man in the wheelchair. "I did suggest we do it right away."

"Quite," agreed Peter.

Joan intervened. "I thought we had all agreed at Monday's meeting to wait until Felicity returned. That, as you all know, was the Colonel's preference. He doesn't really see why the police should be called in, if we can sort this out amongst ourselves."

"I'm not sure that we all agree with that," Peter complained. "Anyway, shouldn't it be reported to the Management Committee?".

The sofa felt crowded, and Felicity desperately wanted to escape. Her heart was beating sixty to the dozen; she tried to slow her breathing while staring fixedly at her hands. Suddenly everyone was standing up and regrouping; bidding each other farewell; shaking hands (no bisous here) and agreeing to meet again on Monday. It was also made very apparent to Felicity that she was not invited. She walked out of that flat in a daze, but the firm hand of John took hold of her and guided her towards his door.

"Come in, Felicity," John said.

"Flic, please. I never go by Felicity, I'm not sure why everyone here seems to insist on calling me that."

John's eyes told her that he knew precisely why.

"Take a seat, Flic. That armchair's the comfiest, but you'll have to turf the cat off first."

"But I thought pets…"

John raised his eyebrows in question, and Felicity immediately understood that this man was a rebel; she began to relax as she decided to sit elsewhere. It hardly seemed fair to the cat to do otherwise. John had discarded his original tweedy look and was dressed in a denim shirt and red corduroy slacks, unlike his other neighbours in their dowdy jackets and ties. With his thick dark hair, and warm brown eyes, she thought that, for an older man, he looked quite fanciable. But then she remembered that she, of course, was older too.

"I reckon we both need a drink after that debacle. Are you the sherry type, or would you prefer a glass of wine? Maybe even a whisky?"

"A glass of wine would be heavenly."

"You're not into whisky as an aperitif then," John observed, as he began to uncork a bottle of claret. "I must say I've always believed it to be a very odd French habit. They tell me you were living there until recently. Whereabouts?"

Felicity took a large gulp of red wine and tried to breathe more steadily. But she wasn't sure if she really felt like making chit chat with this man. Her anger was rising and, try as she might, she couldn't keep calm. She took a second gulp to see if that would help. John seemed to understand. He leaned over to stroke the cat, a lovely grey Persian, and then stood up. Pulling a vinyl record from its sleeve, he began to clean it with a special duster, turning it over and over between his hands. Then bending down, he slotted it onto the turntable of his stereo player, lifted the stylus with his forefinger, and placed it with infinite care onto the spinning record. The cool, sultry brass notes of Miles Davis playing 'Kind of Blue' spread like incense around the room. Was this old chap trying to seduce her?

"There are a few details, Flic, that I think I should fill you in on: about who you can really trust, that sort of thing. Tell me, how long is it since you were last in Dunborough? You must find things very different nowadays."

"But what... how do you...?"

"You mean you haven't realised? Oh dear, I must be confusing you. I'm afraid I never forget a face, but it's pretty obvious to me now that you don't even remember me. I'm so sorry."

"Oh God, it's me who should be apologising... I...

131

umm…" Felicity was frantically trying to figure out where she had met this man before. Yes, she realised, there was definitely something familiar about him: that small stoop that masked his height, that slightly teasing smile.

"Miss Jones." He was offering her a clue now. "Newly appointed teacher at Sunnyvale School."

Felicity still couldn't place him. None of those stuffy male teachers had looked a jot like him. And anyway, he would have been much much younger then, as she had been. Her male colleagues had seemed ancient. No, she still didn't have a clue. Perhaps his display of photographs, meticulously arranged along the polished mahogany top of an upright piano, might help.

"Would you mind if I looked at your photographs?" she asked.

"No, go ahead."

She stood up so that she could examine them more closely. A portrait of a young graduate took centre stage. He was dressed in a gown and mortar board, and flanked by two older people whom Felicity presumed to be his parents. He held a rolled white diploma between his hands like a sergeant at arms.

"Mrs Cherry," Felicity exclaimed. "Oh my goodness… it's Mrs Cherry, our wonderful school welfare assistant." She turned towards John. "So, Mrs Cherry was your mother?"

John just grinned.

She fell silent before suddenly announcing, "You

know I really loved her. She was so kind to me, just like she was kind to all the children at that place."

John lowered his eyes.

"I'd love to meet her again. Is she still…?"

He shook his head. "She died back in 2003 at the age of eighty. Not long after my dad."

"Oh, I'm so sorry. Do you know she invited me for supper, shortly after I had arrived in Dunborough. I think she recognised that I was a lost soul. None of the teachers were that welcoming. She was full of stories about you, about your travels in India and your passage through medical school. She was so proud."

"She told me all about you too. I think she wanted to pair us up, but that was never going to be. We did meet briefly though, do you remember?"

Felicity did remember now. He had come to the school nativity play, which was where they had been introduced. But she couldn't remember talking to him for long. She was examining more photographs now: John in mountaineering gear; John on a sailing dinghy; John in his primary school uniform. Then she turned away from the piano to examine two further photographs that stood alongside each other on an adjacent glass coffee table. Each image recorded a loving couple, and each was housed in a silver frame. The first depicted an older Mr and Mrs Cherry. The moment Felicity looked at it, she grew flustered and quickly turned away to look at the second portrait. But that one confused her too. It revealed two older men, standing shoulder to shoulder, each sporting a white jacket and colourful bow tie.

"My husband, Bill," John explained. "We both practised medicine in Malawi, and then we moved to London together. We finally married at Paddington back in 2014, not long before he became ill. I decided to retire to Dunborough after he died."

Felicity tried to summon some appropriate words, but remained silent, finally mumbling, "I'm so sorry." In truth she half wondered whether she wasn't feeling slightly miffed.

"That's enough about me. Tell me a little more about you, Miss Jones."

Their conversation continued long into the evening. They shared the rest of the bottle of wine and John produced some cheese and biscuits which helped to stave off Felicity's mounting hunger. At last she had found a fellow enthusiast for her beloved Roquefort. Her neighbour tactfully avoided the subject of the theft until Felicity decided that it was time to leave. Then he reintroduced it.

"Flic... I fully understand how angry you must be feeling. I mean over what they are saying about your cleaner."

"Gloria," Felicity corrected him. "She's much more than a cleaner, she's a friend."

"I don't for a moment believe it was her, trust me. Look, there are things you should know, but now is not the time. I gather Gloria comes every Sunday, am I right?"

"Yes, she does now. She helped me a lot though, during my first weeks here."

"Well, you're going to have to explain to her what has happened."

"Oh God," Felicity groaned. "It's going to be really tough. Look, John, I don't care what anyone is saying. I know for a fact that she didn't steal that Picasso."

"Flic, I honestly don't doubt it."

"It's funny how no one wanted her to have that key." They both fell silent. Then Felicity took a breath and announced, "You know I'm beginning to hate this country. It just feels so… so… hostile."

"Don't," was all he said. There was a long silence before John spoke again. "We're not all like that, Flic, even if it seems hard to believe, what with Brexit and everything else that has happened recently. I firmly believe that the rest of us have got to stick together." He looked intently into her eyes, making Felicity feel even more confused. "Just let me warn you now. Take great care when you deal with the Colonel. He's a nasty bit of work."

"Thanks for the advice, John. And thanks for the wine. It's been… er… nice… really really nice to find a good neighbour at last."

"You don't remember him, do you?"

"Who? Oh, the Colonel? No, should I?"

"George Evans? Mr Evans?"

Felicity was racking her brain.

"He may style himself as a colonel," John continued. "You'll see that he's even grown a moustache to look the part. But he's never worn a uniform in his life."

"Mr Evans?" Felicity repeated slowly. "Mis... ter... Evans... not...?"

"Yes," John said with an air of satisfaction. "That Mr Evans... Sports Master at Sunnyvale School. Not a man to meddle with."

Tina
Wood Terrace, Dunborough, England
November 5th 2017

Tina had been plaiting Alice's hair in cornrows again that morning, but this time her granddaughter had been unusually fidgety. Most probably because she'd been promised a few fireworks in the garden before bedtime. Nothing dangerous of course, just a few sparklers mainly.

Winston had taken her to the park about an hour ago now, but as soon as everyone got back, they were going to have chicken, rice and peas for lunch, with a Bakewell tart and jug of Bird's custard she had made for afters. Tina wished she could do more to help and felt pretty useless. It was hurtful that Gloria was having to pay all the food bills until they could sort everything out with the dratted Home Office. In her mind, her old boss owed her a big apology, and should be begging her to return to work. After all, assuming she could go back some time, when and if this was all sorted out, she was going to have to work until she was sixty-six before she could collect her state pension. That had come as a big shock at the time. Hadn't she already paid a fortune into their scheme? But then what use would that be to her if they sent her back to Jamaica. She doubted that she would ever see that money again. The way the Home Office were dragging their feet, they might well be deporting her, whatever their MP was saying to the contrary.

"Hi Mum, it's only me," shouted Gloria as she let herself in the front door.

Tina heard her feet on the stairs and smiled. She was going to miss her old city flat, but in many ways it was good to be all together again, and her daughter's new job was very good news indeed. As for that stuck-up bitch white woman she'd just been to see, well, Tina didn't trust her one jot.

Pulling the chicken out of the oven to check it, she decided it was time to heat up the rice and peas from yesterday. Hopefully Alice and Winston would be back soon too.

Ten minutes later, she took the rice and peas off the stove and turned down the oven. Alice must have been reluctant to leave the park, for she and Winston had still not arrived back. All was quiet from Gloria's room.

She called gently up the stairs. "Gloria, baby love, you coming down soon?"

"I'm not hungry, Mum. I think I'll give lunch a miss," Gloria called back.

Tina paused. She'd been here before many times

when her daughter was a troubled teen, but what on earth was going on now? Gloria was her rock. She mounted the stairs and tapped on the door before pushing it open. There was her beloved daughter, sitting on the edge of her bed, staring furiously at the floor.

"I told you I'm not coming down, Mum," Gloria stated angrily.

Tina sat down beside her. Ten minutes later, after Gloria had explained everything, Tina took a breath.

"That's how things are for us, honey, and always will be. These whites think they own the world. *Who us?*" she mimicked. "*No, we're not prejudiced! Racism? In this country?* My God, they have no idea. They don't know what it's like for us. They're never the ones at the sharp end of police violence."

"Aw, Mum. We've got to get on with each other. This is their country after all."

"No, Gloria honey, it's our country. It's for me, you, Winston and Alice too, and don't forget it. If they hadn't wanted us here in the first place, they should never have taken us away from our own countries and sold us as slaves. I don't suppose they talked a lot about that in your history lessons at school."

"Aw, Mum. You sound just like Joseph. We can't keep on being angry. It just eats you up. We've got to move on."

"Huh!" Tina continued to fume. "That's all very well. But you know as well as I do, Gloria, that we're never going to be treated as equals. As soon as a white policeman sees a couple of black kids with something in their pockets, he's searching them for drugs. As soon as something goes missing at your posh establishment, it's the brown lady who took it. Who else could it have possibly been?"

"Aw, Mum."

"I just don't understand what possessed you to work for that stupid bitch."

"But, Mum, she's not at all like you say... she's doing her best to sort this out."

"You sure of that honey? I'm pretty sure I saw your precious lady in the park the other day. If she was the one you've been telling me about, I wouldn't give her an inch."

"Mum, what ya' talkin' about?"

"Just ask her what she knows about Sunnyvale School. Go on. If you're ever mad enough to get in touch with her again, just ask her."

"Mum... be reasonable."

Tina had turned away from her daughter and was staring angrily through the window. But Gloria persisted.

"I suppose I kinda knew that she must have been a teacher once. But if she was, she's changed since then. Honestly, if you met her, you'd like her."

"Baby love, you wouldn't catch me within a mile of that place of hers. And if you've any sense, you'll keep clear of it too."

Now Gloria fell silent for a while. "You know, Mum,

I'm scared," she confessed. "Some of them want to call the police."

"Gloria, you're innocent. You've not got nothin' to fear."

"I know that really, but…" Gloria paused, as if she were considering whether to say more. "Someone…" she suddenly blurted out, "the Colonel, of all people, said he saw me leaving last Sunday with a big carrier bag. It was Felicity's duvet cover and things. I was bringing them home to iron. But they said I must be carrying that bleedin' bowl in it."

"So what? You know for a fact you weren't! You don't have nothing to worry about. Look, you don't never have to go back to that awful place. You didn't take their poncy bowl and that's that."

"Mum, I've got to see this through. If I don't, then they'll say I did it… no question." Just then Gloria's phone rang. "It's Flic," she informed her quickly.

Tina watched as all sorts of emotions played across her daughter's beloved face in the space of a few seconds: astonishment and delight were quickly followed by a look of despair.

"What is it ,what is it?" she demanded to know.

She could hear Felicity's voice echoing from the phone, strident and bossy. Some people never change, she thought bitterly.

Gloria held her mobile away from her ear for a second and whispered to her mum, "They've found the bowl."

But then her smile quickly faded. Tina could hear Felicity talking excitedly on the other end, but something was definitely up with Gloria. Finally, her daughter spoke into the phone in a slow whisper.

"Flic, I'm afraid there's something I didn't tell you." Tina groaned. "God, Flic, I'm so sorry. I feel so bloody foolish," she sniffed. "When I got there last Sunday morning the case wasn't properly closed. There was no one around, so I lifted the bowl out to have a better look at it. I was really, really careful, I promise you. I just wanted to check it out, to see what it felt like to hold."

Felicity's response was fainter now, and Tina noticed a faint smile cross Gloria's face.

"Thanks Flic," she said. "I knew you'd understand. Believe me Flic, it was like magic. It's so so beautiful, it really is."

Tina was looking at her daughter in astonishment now. She'd never seen her like this before. Was she going a bit soft in the head?

"My God Flic," Gloria continued. "Do you realise, if they do call the police, they're going to find my fingerprints all over it."

Whatever Felicity said next didn't seem to bring Gloria any relief.

"Thanks for understanding, Flic, but I feel I've just gone and brought you lots of hassle."

Felicity spoke again.

"OK Flic," Gloria sniffed.

"Tell her you're not going back," Tina urged, pulling

anxiously at her sleeve.

Gloria turned away in annoyance. "OK, Flic," she continued, trying to laugh. "It's agreed. We're not going to let those bastards grind us down. By the way, do you still want me to come next Sunday?" There was a pause. "Aw thanks Flic. Thank you."

When Gloria looked up from the phone, her mum was staring at her in amazement.

"*Thanks Flic, thank you*?" she mocked. "What the hell you ingratiating yourself with that white woman for. Don't think for a second that you can trust her. She's just like all the rest."

*

Tina was busy seeing her granddaughter into bed. Alice had showered, cleaned her teeth and was now pulling her pyjama top over her head.

"Did you enjoy the fireworks, honey?"

"They were really cool, Nana. Can we have a bonfire as well next year? Amy said they'd built one in her garden and she and her cousin had to make a guy to go on the top."

"We'll see, honey. It's up to your mum really. The garden's a little small. Now hop into bed. You've got school tomorrow."

"I don't like school anymore."

"What? You told me you loved school and that Mrs Macmillan was the best teacher ever."

"But Amy's not allowed to play with me."

"What? Who said that?"

"Her dad."

"Well, honey, in my mind, if Amy wants to play with you, she should, whatever her dad says. He's just a big nincompoop."

Alice giggled.

"And if she doesn't want to play with you, then there are plenty of other children who will, because I know you're the loveliest girl in the world, and so do they."

Tina tucked the duvet firmly around her and leaned in for a kiss. She was met by a warm cloud of lemon scented soap; she inhaled deeply. How she had dreamed of that smell during those long, lonely nights at Copse Hill.

She descended the stairs slowly, deep in thought. If she had her way all schools would be abolished. They were hateful places. The only time she had ever enjoyed studying was after she'd left school, when learning was no longer compulsory. By that time people had begun to treat her with respect. But as for that school for dummies that they had sent her to straight after she had arrived from Jamaica, well, there they just treated her like dirt. She only had to open her mouth to say something, and they'd tell her she was being rude and cheeky. Some of the teachers she had weren't too bad, but that Mr Evans, he was violent. Most of those boys, poor souls, wouldn't hurt a flea. But she'd seen Mr Evans hitting them over the head on more than one occasion. She had quickly learned that it wasn't worth trying to say something, because then he'd just take it out on you. The sitting room door lay open at the bottom of the stairs, so she poked her head round to see what her daughter was doing. Gloria was sitting on the sofa watching *Antiques Roadshow*, so Tina decided to make them both a cup of tea and join her.

"Here you are, honey. You feeling more cheerful now?"

"Thanks, Mum. Yeah, sorry for being a misery earlier. Did you put my sweetener in?"

Tina nodded and they both sipped pensively for a moment.

"I like him," Gloria commented as Ronnie Archer Morgan eulogised over some piece of African tribal art. "Makes a change to see someone who's black."

Tina wasn't so sure. "Hmm. Could do with a few more black faces around on the telly if you ask me."

"Aw, Mum."

"What you decide about going back to that place next Sunday?"

"Flic said the others are having a meeting on Monday. She promised to get in touch with me afterwards. We're going to go from there."

"I'm not going to say another thing."

"Then don't. I'm up to here with it all. You haven't told Alice about it, have you?"

"No, honey, of course not."

"I won't be able to think straight at work tomorrow.

I pray to God it doesn't get back to them."

Tina had been going to tell her about Amy's dad but decided that now was not the right time.

"Mum, what did you mean when you said I should ask Flic about Sunnyvale? She wasn't really a teacher there, was she?"

"You'd better ask her about that. All I can say is that if she is who I think she is, she let me down badly. She was one of the only teachers I could really trust at that goddam stinking hole. Then she went all funny and turned against me. Next thing I knew she'd gone and left."

Felicity
Avon Court, Dunborough, England
November 5th 2017

"The thing is…" John was saying as they sat in Felicity's flat later that evening, "he's a wily bastard."

John had dropped by to see how Felicity was feeling after her meeting with Gloria earlier.

"We'll have to play him at his own game. I'm one hundred percent certain that it is our precious Colonel who is stirring things up. I was at that meeting when they objected to Gloria having her own key, and he was verging on racist slander. But try suggesting it to any of the others. Either they think that he's the cat's whiskers or they're too scared of him to rock the boat."

"Frankly, I hope I never cross his path again. I remember he used to scare the living daylights out of me, not to mention the kids. Thanks for coming round to talk it over before your meeting tomorrow."

"I assume you had a long talk with Gloria. How did she take it?"

"She's mortified, extremely upset. You know, I

remember when someone's watch went missing at my grammar school. We all had to lift our desk lids so that the teacher could search for it. I distinctly recall blushing and quaking with fear. It was almost as if I really believed I was the culprit. God, I really feel for Gloria. It's all my fault."

"Would you have acted like that teacher, Miss Jones?"

"Certainly not. It was utterly cruel."

They chuckled, then jumped in their seats as a loud crack startled them and a whoosh of coloured sparks rose above the edge of the balcony.

"They must be starting the display at the recreation ground. We should get a good view of the fireworks from here. Grab your coat, Flic."

They both zipped up, slid open the patio door and stepped outside onto the balcony.

"I love fireworks, don't you?"

"Not half," Felicity exulted, as a series of rockets shot skywards, releasing thousands of stars in a succession of pink, silver and gold. "I just wish they would soften those bangs. It sounds like there's a war going on. Or am I just an old fogey?"

"You're as young as you feel," John shouted above the noise of the next rocket, "if you'll pardon the cliché."

At that moment Felicity felt very young indeed. After the last sparks had spluttered to the ground, they retired inside.

"Well, I've had a long day," John apologised, "and I suppose I really ought to get back to check on Smokey. It's as well I remembered to keep him in."

"Doesn't anyone object to you having a cat?"

"What cat? He just pays me a visit via my balcony from time to time." His eyes sparkled with mischief for a moment before his expression turned more serious. "Look, I'll report back after tomorrow's meeting. You really mustn't worry. The two of us are going to sort this out."

"Thanks, John. Do you mind if I ask you a question before you go?"

They had reached the door, and John turned to face her again.

"Not at all. Fire ahead."

"Your mum. In that photograph, the one with your father, when they were older. She was wearing a sari. Was she...?"

"Indian? Yes. You didn't realise? My dad had been working out in India as a civil servant. That's where he and Mum met. She was a member of the Anglo Indian Community in fact, many of whom left shortly after partition. She was always very sad about that. I was born the year after they arrived in the UK."

"But why didn't she wear her sari more often? She looked so beautiful."

"She certainly was very very beautiful. You know, now that I am back in Dunborough, I miss her more than ever."

"But why? Why did I never see her in it?"

"Don't you know? I think you do, Flic. I think you
know only too well."

Felicity
Avon Court, Dunborough, England
November 6th 2017

"Flic, it's John. I hope it's not too late to call."

"Hi. I've been waiting for you to get in touch. How did the meeting go?"

"I don't know quite how to tell you. Look, I'm a bit wound up, so I'm going to have a walk to calm myself down. Would it be a bit much for me to ask if you would come with me?"

"I'll get my coat and meet you at the door in five."

"Thanks, Flic."

When they hit the outside, Felicity felt pleased that she had thought to wear a hat, and immediately wrapped her cashmere scarf more firmly around her neck. A neon fog swirled above the weir and their breath hung on the air as they spoke.

"Where were you planning to go?"

"I often come out here at this time in the evening. How about we follow the river out of town? With that full moon, we shouldn't have a problem seeing where we're going."

They set off in silence and soon left the weir behind. After a while the sound of rushing water had diminished and the river became their silent companion. A car suddenly intruded as it sped past them on an adjacent road, but before long all sounds of traffic had vanished, and the gentle hooting of a male tawny owl was the only sign of life.

"There's a bench a little bit further on," John said eventually. "Shall we stop there and have a rest before we go back?"

They sat side by side facing the water. Endless silvery fish darted past them as the river slipped by under the moonlight. Felicity began to wonder if John was ever going to speak again.

"It's blackmail," he blurted out suddenly, finally releasing the tension that surrounded them both. "It's blackmail, pure and simple."

"How do you mean?"

"That lot. Honestly, Flic, they're just a bunch of creeps. They let George Evans get away with murder." It was a while before he spoke again. "George Evans says he knows for certain that your cleaner... sorry... his words... stole that bowl. But then she got scared and put it back. He says that if you don't get that key back and give her the push, they should go to the police. He's implying that there's something missing from his flat too, though God knows how Gloria is meant to have got in there."

"And what do the others say about that?"

"They're all in total agreement with him. You know, Flic, I think I've completely lost my faith in human nature. Can't they see what a duplicitous man he is?"

Felicity felt stunned. Surely, this all went against natural justice. "Do you really mean to tell me that they're not even prepared to consider the possibility that Gloria is innocent?"

Now it was Felicity's turn to command silence. She needed time to think. She wondered whether to tell John about Gloria handling the ceramic but decided that would just complicate everything right now. Still, of one thing she felt absolutely certain. She admired John's integrity and would put her total trust in whatever he suggested that they should do. He was Mrs Cherry's son, after all.

When they returned home, Felicity gazed up at their apartment building while John fumbled in the pocket of his cords for his key. Lights blazed a welcome from some windows, while at others, curtains were firmly drawn. The top floor seemed to be in total darkness, but then a sudden flash of light escaped briefly as a curtain was held aside, causing Felicity to feel a chill of apprehension. The Colonel, it would seem, was watching them from his penthouse flat. In spite of John's warming arm around her shoulder, she shivered.

During all the years that Felicity had spent alone in France after Alistair's death, she had rarely felt afraid at night. But this evening, that nagging fear stayed with her, and she checked twice over that all doors and windows were firmly locked before she went to bed. But sleep was obviously going to evade her that night. She lay awake, alert to any extraneous sound, turning everything over and over in her mind. It hadn't surprised her one bit to learn that Mr Evans was behind the attack on Gloria. Indeed, this tactic had an air of familiarity.

As the night progressed, she began to reflect more deeply on her time at Sunnyvale School, unearthing hurtful memories that she had buried deeper than the deepest tomb. It was hard to believe that she was the same person as she had been back then: that opinionated yet naïve young girl who had taken up a coveted appointment and planned to become the greatest and wisest special needs teacher of all time. She felt sure now that, while some people had been exceedingly kind to her, others must have felt resentful of her pompous optimism.

Just before dawn broke, Felicity fell into a troubled sleep. But it wasn't pleasant trying to doze when people kept trying to look at you, pushing and shoving each other to get to the front, and bringing their heads low towards the pillow while breathing into your face. There was Miss Williams from domestic science who had always been so kind. But her breath was sour now and her eyes narrow. She was linking arms with Mrs Burton, the needlework teacher, who just snorted in disgust and pulled her friend away.

"What's she doing there?" a male voice barked. "I

always said she was lazy."

Felicity whimpered. She had believed Mr Padman to be supportive.

"Useless," a voice came from the back.

"Above her station, if you ask me," said another.

Felicity tried to protest, but her throat felt constricted. Mrs Potter, the vicar's wife, was poking her now with a ruler, digging her in the ribs and whacking it over her skull so hard that her head ached. She wormed her way to the other side of the bed, only to find the school secretary, the spitting image of Joan, staring up at her from the pillow. Sweating profusely now and struggling to free her limbs from the constraining duvet, she cowered against the padded bed head as at least twenty angry white faces advanced towards her.

But one person stood out from the crowd. She just shook her head sadly from side to side saying, "Such a pity, such a pity. I never would have believed it." It was Mrs Cherry.

Suddenly, Alexa was declaring that it was seven-thirty and Minou seemed to be scratching at the door. As she swung her legs over the edge of the bed to go and let him in, she realised that there was no Minou, and there was no door. Meanwhile the hostile teachers had vanished with the light.

Felicity
The Minstrel Inn, Dunborough, England
November 7th 2017

"How long have you got?" Felicity asked as they sat down at a table close to the fire.

"Not long, I'm afraid," Gloria answered. "I'm supposed to be back by one."

"What're you having to drink? Surely you've got time to eat a sandwich? What would you like, cheese, chicken or ham?"

As Felicity stood at the bar waiting for attention, she smiled ruefully as she thought of the long sacrosanct lunch breaks that all workers used to take in France. People expected too much from their staff nowadays in her opinion. Felicity gave her order and returned to her seat.

"You know I do love a real fire. Pity I can't have one in my apartment," she said as she settled onto the bench opposite her friend.

Gloria didn't seem to have registered her return and was lost in thought. Finally, she took a deep breath and spoke with a rush.

"Flic. Mum says I'd be absolutely mad to go back to your place. I've been giving it a lot of thought ever since our conversation on Sunday. The last thing I want to do is let you down, but you know I think she's right. I've got a good job now at the art shop. I don't need more work. And just imagine if the police did get involved. It scares my mum stiff even though I've done nothing wrong. She says they're biased against black people." She exhaled deeply and seemed close to tears. "Look, I'm really sorry, Flic."

Felicity rested her hand on Gloria's. "Gloria love, you really don't have to apologise. In fact," she ventured, suddenly brightening, "you're doing me a favour. I have every intention of doing my own cleaning from now on. It'll keep me supple. I might even get a robot to help me and we can do the Roomba together."

"Are you really sure you don't mind?"

"What sort of person do you think I am? Why should I mind? It's I who should be apologising to you for my excruciatingly awful neighbours. I can't say you didn't warn me."

Gloria raised a smile.

"Anyway, I'm delighted you have a new job: one that you like. And you know I also think your mum's probably right. We've all heard of cases where black people have been prosecuted unfairly. Just look at what happens in America. I've heard of cases where people of colour have been jailed for years and they were totally

157

innocent. God knows how many may still be in jail."

Gloria shuddered. "Well, you wouldn't expect that sort of thing to happen in England," she said.

Felicity raised her eyebrows. "Don't be too sure about that. Look, here are our drinks."

"Mum seems to think she knows you. Did you used to teach at Sunnyvale?"

Felicity had been hoping that she would never be asked this question. "Well actually, Gloria, yes, I did. But I was a very different person back then. Didn't you say your mum was called Tina?"

"Yes. She came over here in '68 and left school in '73 when she was sixteen."

"Then I did know her. I wasn't there long. The school didn't suit me, or should I say, I wasn't the right person for that job. I left at the end of '72. And I do remember teaching a young girl from Jamaica called Tina."

"Hmm."

"It would be really nice if your mum and I could meet. What do you think? You know she wrote me the most amazing poem once. I don't think I ever told her how good it was. She was a clever girl, your mum."

"I know she was. God knows why they sent her to a 'special' school."

"I do. There was this misguided notion that people who spoke Jamaican patois were inferior beings. I imagine it was quite a culture shock for her when she first arrived here."

"She won't never see you, Flic. She says she

158

wouldn't meet up with you if you were the last person alive. I'm sorry, Flic, but she thinks you're a stuck-up bitch."

Felicity gasped, and Gloria half giggled an apology.

"Do you agree with your mum?"

"No, Flic. You know I don't. I wish I hadn't told you now. Look, I've brought the key back. Here, please take it." Gloria hastily slapped it down onto the table where it seemed to take on an ominous presence. "Go on, take it back," she urged. "If you do, then that bastard Colonel shouldn't cause us any more trouble."

Felicity looked reluctant. "It's not right," she said. "It's like he's won." The key remained in place. "Do you know that he was a teacher once at Sunnyvale. He's never seen military service in his life."

Gloria looked astounded. "Go on. I don't believe it."

"He must have been desperate to get out of teaching because, apparently, he borrowed to buy a couple of new builds. Then, once property prices started to go up, he was able to re-mortgage and buy more. Now he's got tenants all over Dunborough, and probably elsewhere for all I know."

"I can't wait to tell my friend… the one I told you about; that colonel fellow is her landlord. She's scared stiff of him. Do you know he even threatened to evict her because she went on housing benefit? She'll think this is an absolute scream."

Felicity couldn't see the funny side at all. If she had been falsely maligned by this man, as Gloria had been, she wouldn't be amused one tiny little bit.

*

"This is becoming a habit," John declared.

Felicity was busy pouring drinks in the kitchen. "What is?" she called back.

"You and me."

Felicity bent down to replace the bottle in the fridge and hovered underneath the counter for a second to cool her cheeks and compose herself. Then she gathered the glasses and walked around to John who was sitting in an armchair. The curtains had not yet been drawn and the lights from the town were playing gaudily over the water.

"You know I never tire of this view," he said as he reached up to take a glass from her. "Thank you."

Felicity took her place on the sofa, desperately trying to conceal her embarrassment. It wasn't her usual style to go running after men and she certainly hadn't wanted to give him the wrong idea. But then she couldn't deny that she was the one who had rung this evening asking whether they could meet again. She sighed. His presence did feel enormously comforting, and there were things from last night's dream that needed untangling.

"So, this dream? You said it was troubling you."

Felicity tried a laugh to remove the tension, but he seemed serious, earnest even. Her new sofa suddenly felt like a psychiatrist's couch.

"Tell me about it," he insisted, leaning forward. She had to admit, John did have a wonderful bedside manner.

"Oh, I'm sure it'll sound utterly trivial to you. You must be sick and tired of hearing about Gloria and our little problems."

John placed a firm hand on her arm. "Flic," he reassured her, "where racism and unfairness are concerned, it certainly isn't trivial. Now what's up?"

"John, did your mum ever say anything about me?"

"Of course she did. I told you. She wanted us..."

"I mean..." She paused. "Did she ever say anything negative? Tell me the truth, John, please."

If this was a real psychiatrist's session, she would now be reaching for that man-size box of tissues that would have been discreetly placed at her disposal. But she had never been the crying sort. She hadn't even cried back then when all the staff had seemed to turn against her. Those last months at Sunnyvale School had been some of the loneliest in her life. And now last night's dream had brought it all back. Suddenly, for no apparent reason, all her teaching colleagues had turned hostile. Even the people whom she had considered as friends had snubbed her. Now, nearly fifty years later, as she was gently cruising towards old age, her repressed memories were resurfacing, and she was about to open the lock gates.

John was rubbing his hand over his chin as he sat deep in thought. He hadn't shaved that morning, which stirred Felicity slightly.

"She did say something about a tape recorder I seem to remember," he said at last. "Did it go missing perhaps?"

"A tape recorder? Yes, there was one, and yes, it did go missing. I used it for recording my children's conversations. But then it turned up again suddenly, right out of the blue. I thought I must have been going mad. Why... what did your mum say about it?"

John was now rubbing his thumb rapidly backwards and forwards across his chin. A faint rasping noise filled the embarrassing silence that followed. He seemed to be avoiding her eyes as she searched his face trying to understand what lay behind his question. She could still picture the small rectangular tape recorder that she had positioned on her desk all those years ago. Hardly state of the art nowadays, but it *was* back then. She had found it indispensable. She remembered how her kindly headmistress had accorded her an afternoon's leave every week, so that she could pursue her studies at a local university.

Felicity's main interest lay in language in education, and she and her fellow students were set the task of recording their children's speech. They were to select a piece to transcribe and submit to the tutor. Felicity had felt inspired and set up this very cassette recorder on her desk so that she could follow these instructions. But some of her fellow students taught in elite schools and she worried about how her selected piece might be received. After all, most of her children could not even form a complete or comprehensible English sentence. She needed to give them a focus to help them communicate, so Felicity gave every pupil a coloured wine bottle to look through and set about recording their reactions. It had worked beautifully. Her stumbling hesitant pupils began to chatter away to themselves, albeit often incoherently. Billy, a lad of around ten years of age, had become entranced. As his face emerged from behind the bottle, his eyes had shone through his ultra-thick glasses. His excited babbling was hard to comprehend, but Felicity had recorded him. Later she had set about analysing and transcribing his words. When she had finished, she discovered that Billy had created poetry.

"It's like a jelly on a wobble plate, Miss, all green and blue, like... like you're under the water with the fishes, Miss, and seaweed and things."

Felicity hadn't a clue what the others would think of this and wondered whether to feel proud or embarrassed when her linguistics professor selected Billy's words to share with the group. He had asked her to bring the original tape recording the next time they met. Two days later she fell sick and had to take a few days off school. But when she returned to her classroom, the tape recorder was nowhere to be seen. After Felicity had explained all this to John, he said quietly.

"I remember it all now. Mum was most upset. I'd come back from med school for the weekend and she told me that everyone was saying that you had stolen it."

"And did she believe that too?"

"No, Flic. I don't think she did at heart. But then she couldn't make sense of it either. When she tried to defend you, people told her she was too good hearted."

"That was exactly how she was, John." Felicity smiled. "She wouldn't believe ill of anyone."

"But listen, Flic. Let's play detectives for a minute. You say it suddenly turned up again?"

"Yes, but it was absolutely horrible when it did. This is why I needed to talk to you."

"What do you mean?"

"I'd gone down to the staffroom a bit late for my coffee one morning and nearly all the staff were already there. When I went through the door, everyone fell silent. It was as if I had grown two heads or something. I could feel everyone staring at me."

"So, what did you do?"

"I just went ahead and made myself a cup of coffee. Instant... ugh... I don't know how I could have ever drunk that stuff. Then as I turned around, there it was... the tape recorder I mean... sitting on the table, all neatly wrapped up in newspaper. I could tell what it was from the size and shape."

"So?"

"So I just laughed and said brightly 'oh good, it's

been found'."

"And what did they say?"

"Nothing that I can remember. It just felt so creepy. No one said a thing. But I knew for certain that they were all watching me to see how I reacted."

"You poor soul. It sounds grim. So, what did you do next?"

"Oh, it's such a long time ago, John. I don't exactly remember. I think I probably just downed my coffee and left."

There was a long silence. As the abbey bells began to chime the hour, John spoke once more.

"Do you see any coincidences between then and now, Flic?" he asked. "I know I certainly do."

"Hmm," Felicity pondered. "Yes, I think I do. Someone had set a trap for me, hadn't they? Then they went about stirring up all the others." Felicity still felt a nauseous feeling in the pit of her stomach as she recalled that day. Until this moment she hadn't shared this feeling of embarrassment and shame with anyone.

"And if this same person who set you up has now set a trap for Gloria, then it can only be…"

"George Evans," they both exclaimed together.

"But what I will never understand is why he, or anyone else for that matter, would do that to me."

"Did he have any reason for resenting you? I can't imagine how anyone could not have loved you, but then George Evans was, and still is, an out and out misogynist."

Felicity felt herself blushing... which was utterly ridiculous at her age. "Well... yes," she said slowly. "I suppose they all might have resented me in a way. I wasn't very tactful in those days and I am sure I made it clear I didn't think much of their teaching methods... at least with some of them."

"Oh, Flic," John admonished.

"I know, John. I was a right..." She stopped, for John had never known her to be indelicate. "But I *was*," she said lamely. "I was pretty tactless." She continued to reflect. "Oh yes, and there's something else too... maybe some of my colleagues resented the free afternoon I had off school every week. Mrs Harris certainly wasn't obliged to grant me it."

"You didn't lose pay?"

"No. She was really supportive."

"Mum told me she thought a lot of you."

"Well clearly they didn't all think the same way."

*

Later that evening, Felicity was preparing to go to bed. She checked all the locks twice over. She even checked inside the fitted bedroom cupboards and underneath her overly large bed before climbing in. A sleeping pill accompanied by a large crystal tumbler of water awaited her on the bedside cabinet. That night all dreams were to be banished. She'd had enough of being poked and prodded with rulers and bashed about the head with heavy books. But as she reached for her glass, the silent bedroom was suddenly riven by a resounding yell.

"That's it! I get it now! Why, oh why, didn't I see it before."

Was she imagining it, or were the abbey bells really ringing out to celebrate with her as she whooped with joy? For suddenly everything was falling into place. Now Felicity knew exactly what kind of man she was dealing with, and this victim was going to seek her revenge. She would need John's support, but she knew he would be on board. She intended to finally expose that hideous man as the vile, vituperative and racist misogynist that he had proven himself to be.

Felicity
Avon Court, Dunborough, England
November 8th 2017

"Right. In for a penny, in for a pound as they say."

"What do you plan to say to him? Wouldn't it be a good idea to run it past me first?"

"No, I've given this a lot of thought. Trust me. But I do need you to bear witness so to speak. When you've heard me out, I think you will understand."

The two neighbours had met by arrangement in the entrance hall and were now preparing to mount the two flights of stairs to the penthouse apartment. For some reason the lift never seemed to work beyond the first floor. Felicity waited until she had regained her breath before tapping on the Colonel's door. All was silent from within, and they strained to hear what was going on inside. Felicity tapped again more insistently. They heard shuffling, and when finally the door opened, Felicity was taken aback. The last time that she had encountered George Evans he had been in his early forties. Now, at twice that age, his erstwhile frame had buckled and he walked with a shuffle. His hair had turned a dull reddish grey and was scraped in thin strands over his balding pate. However, his dark brown eyes still shone with the same ferocity beneath bushy red eyebrows, and he now sported a neatly trimmed ginger moustache in true military style.

"What do the two of you want? I don't normally see people who haven't got in touch with me first."

Felicity took an involuntary step back from the threshold when she heard his familiar snarl, but John met her with a firm hand on the small of her back.

"Well, you'd better come in if you have to. I expect it's to inform me about that thief you've been employing. I can't give you long." George Evans shuffled back inside to take a seat in a nearby recliner, leaving his visitors to seat themselves unbidden.

They each pulled a dining chair out from underneath the table and placed them side by side, turning them to face the formidable George Evans. The whole room had a depressing air of neglect, in spite of the opulent furnishings and expansive space, and there was a smell of rotting fruit.

"Well, hurry up about it. What have you come to say? I hope you're going to tell me that black bitch has admitted everything and that you have finally stripped her of the key to our building. Goodness knows why anybody would ever dream of giving it to her in the first place."

Felicity was aghast. Her anger was welling up inside

her and she wanted to wail and shriek at him like a banshee. But she had to stay in control if she were to achieve her aim.

"No, Mr Evans. We haven't come about that at all. Whether she holds the key or not is really none of your business."

"What? How dare you speak to me like that, woman!"

John decided he had better intervene. "There's no need to be rude, George. I think Flic has something important to say to you. Actually, I don't know what it is myself, but I believe it should bring some clarity to this situation. Why don't you go ahead, Flic?"

Felicity had expected to feel nervous, but having seen this ugly sham of a man in his lair, she was raring to go. "I don't know if you remember me, Mr Evans, but I was a fellow teacher of yours at Sunnyvale."

John was scrutinising his face and later reported to Felicity that it was clear he did know her.

"Back in 1972 I happened to be making some tape recordings of my children as part of a language project at the university. I gathered quite a lot of material, some of which I transcribed for my tutor. However, I also recorded some everyday conversations between my children and myself."

"I don't see what this has got to do with me."

"I think you soon will. Do you happen to remember Albert Smith?"

George Evans growled and shook his jowls in contempt.

"Well even if you don't, you will most probably remember what he said on my cassette tape. He said that Mr Evans used to hit him on the head for no reason at all. Sometimes, he said, it really hurt, especially when he used a book. Funny thing is, Mr Evans, some of the other boys agreed with him and said that you frequently hit them too."

"Don't be ridiculous woman. This is slander. Get out of here."

"Flic," John said quietly, putting a hand of restraint on her arm. "I don't quite see where this is leading us."

Felicity gently slid her arm away and continued. "I'll explain. I admit I was young and foolish back then. I didn't dream that anyone would interfere with this tape recorder, and I carelessly left it on my desk, not expecting to fall ill and be absent for a few days. When I returned to work, I reported that the school cassette player had disappeared from my desk."

"What are you prattling on about, woman?"

Felicity ignored Mr Evans and continued. "When the tape recorder could not be found it was imputed that I must have stolen it for my own use at home, to play music and so on. No one actually accused me of it, but it eventually dawned on me that everyone thought as much. A few days afterwards, I was late taking my break, and when I entered the staffroom, every single member of staff, bar Mrs Cherry and the headmistress, were present. There was a strange hush as I entered, and I became aware that everyone was looking at me intently. As I turned towards the table after making myself a cup of coffee, I saw the tape recorder that I had lost, centre stage, so to speak. I reacted with delight, but nobody spoke, and I was left feeling extremely uncomfortable. Someone had obviously been spreading ugly rumours about me before planting it there. Then they had primed everyone to watch my reaction. Would you know who that person was, Mr Evans?"

"If you're trying to smear me you've got another thing coming," George Evans snarled.

"The funny thing was that when I tried to recover my tape, so that I might play the section that I had transcribed for my tutor, I found that it was missing."

John raised his eyebrows as understanding dawned. "Hmm. What do you say to that, George?"

"It's a load of old cobblers," he fumed. "Now just get out of here and take this stupid fancy woman of yours with you."

John didn't budge. Like a forensic lawyer he coolly examined the evidence. "No, George. I'm inclined to believe that Flic is on to something here. It all seems extremely plausible to me. Quite a clever tactic to use if you believe someone might try to malign you, especially if that person holds damning evidence. What is it called nowadays… a sting?"

George Evans' building rage enveloped the room like a storm cloud preceding a hurricane. Felicity leant closer to John. It was just as well that her ex-colleague was physically much diminished.

"Now remind me," John continued. "Where have we seen a similar ruse recently? Didn't something else just happen to turn up out of the blue? Something that had apparently been stolen?"

George Evans had pulled himself out of his chair and was now leaning his hand against it for support. Felicity noticed his stoop and how he had to stop from time to time to suck in more breath as he began to rave.

"How dare you come into my home and accuse me of such things. This is slander. I want you to leave, both of you, and be quick about it. You have no right…"

"Yes, I believe I do have the right, Mr Evans. The right to defend my friend Gloria against blatant and, what's more, illegal racial prejudice. Wouldn't you agree, John?"

"He has form on this one, Flic. It seems that racial prejudice is a speciality of his." John rose from his chair and squared up to face their foe. "Do you know how much you hurt my mother with your barbs and innuendos? She gave up her job at Sunnyvale because of you. She just couldn't take it anymore."

"John, I didn't realise…" Felicity stood alongside him. As she raised her hand to his arm, she noticed that he was shaking.

"Your mother?" George Evans intervened.

"Mrs Cherry, the school welfare assistant."

"She was your mother?" George Evans narrowed his

eyes as he surveyed John anew. "Pah, a mere welfare assistant."

"The life blood of the school and the kindest person there," Felicity intervened. "Sunnyvale would not have been the same without her."

"I believe you understand what I am saying, George," John trembled. Then he paused as if to gather his erstwhile control. "I think we have both made ourselves absolutely clear." John then turned towards his companion. "I think we should leave Mr Evans to reflect on this. I suspect we'll not be hearing any more about it. If he has a shred of decency left, he will be resigning from the Residents' Committee. I know someone who is very competent who can take his place."

George Evans slowly shuffled towards the table which he used for support as he now began to threaten them face to face. "You dare to come here with your childish stories?" he spat. "You have no proof whatsoever. I can assure you that I have the confidence of everyone in this building, and if you persist with these scandalous insinuations, you will both be hearing from my lawyer."

John ignored him and turned away. "Don't worry, Flic," he reassured her, speaking slowly and pointedly. "If George doesn't resign promptly, then the fact that he is not indeed a retired colonel but has more recently made his money as a negligent and cruel landlord may just become more widely known amongst our friends and neighbours."

Seconds later, they were being shown to the door.

"Poofter!" Felicity heard, as the door was slammed behind them. She sincerely hoped that John hadn't heard too.

"Odious man," was all that he said.

Felicity felt like jumping down the stairs two at a time but thought better of it. When they reached their landing, they turned towards each other and gave high fives at exactly the same moment that Joan approached from the end of the corridor. The look on her face made Felicity's day.

Felicity
Avon Court, Dunborough, England
November 20th 2017

Over a week had passed since they had faced up to
George Evans, but as far as Felicity could deduce, the
Colonel still reigned supreme. No resignation had been
offered to the committee, and John reported that
everyone was still talking of Gloria as the supposed
thief. The more Felicity thought about it the more
incensed she became. John had departed for India two
days previously, having formed an attachment to a
children's hospital in Kolkata. It upset her to think that
he would be away for the next two weeks, for now she
would have to bear this all on her own. Who could she
confide in? Gloria had become a friend, but she could
hardly burden her with this, and the less *she* knew about
her hateful neighbour's continuing vendetta the better.
Come hell or high water, Felicity was going to clear her
name.

She decided to concentrate on cleaning her flat that
morning and drive her frustrations away under a cloud

of bleach. Hadn't she vowed to work hard and keep fit when Gloria left? As Felicity bent forward to tackle the limescale on the surface of her bath, her newly acquired robot vacuum cleaner was making its linear progression around the lounge. Later she would work out in the gym before meeting Joan at the pool as arranged. Joan wasn't really so bad after all, and it would be nice to have a chat. As she eased herself upright an image of her mother flashed across the mirror. Dear God, was that old woman really her? She approached the glass with trepidation and began to study her face, as if this were a new and unknown person. Felicity wasn't in the habit of preening herself. She had spent too long with the bleached and botoxed wives of Alistair's American business friends to care too much about wrinkles, having adamantly refused to play the part of a beautiful accessory herself. Anyway, her husband had always said he liked the way she looked.

Nonetheless, Felicity now found herself up against the glass peering anxiously at her unshaped eyebrows and massaging away her newly discovered wrinkles. How could she have let herself go like this? Her normally bright blue eyes looked tired and were set in deep violet folds that revealed her sleeplessness. And what about her hair? It wasn't so much the fact that it was turning grey. She didn't really mind that. It had been fun being the exception in France where women of a certain age liked to dye their hair flame red, constantly compelled to return to the hairdresser to conceal their roots, like puppets on a string. No, she liked to be free of such constraints. But then, she thought, as she pulled at a straying curl, it was certainly time she had a decent cut. Perhaps, by the time that John returned, she might be looking more attractive; a little less haggard.

When Felicity turned up at the swimming pool she was still sweating slightly from the gym and her leotard felt cold and damp against her skin. Joan had discarded her towelling robe and was just tucking the last strands of hair into her flowery rubber swimming hat. Her eyes went wide as she spotted Felicity.

"Oh hi, Joan. I'm a bit behind today," Felicity panted. "I'll see you in the pool."

Before she had finished speaking, the door to the pool had already closed. Joan was swimming lengths as she lowered herself into the tepid water. The vast space hummed with the noise from the filtration system and the overhead fluorescent lighting, while in the corner the Jacuzzi bubbled and burped. Joan was a slow but steady swimmer and Felicity soon caught her up, changing to breaststroke so that they might chat and swim side by side. But her friend only gave her a brief glance before turning away, not seeming too keen on conversation that day. Rolling away, Felicity began to do back crawl instead. After her customary twenty lengths she noticed that the pool was empty. She peered into the changing rooms but they were empty too. This wasn't like the garrulous Joan at all. Felicity decided to jump into the Jacuzzi to mull things over. It didn't make sense. They had met for a swim only the other day, and Joan had been overflowing with gossip. Felicity closed her eyes for a moment. She wasn't going to fret about it, so she lay back to enjoy the feeling of isolation. Perhaps she would ring Alice later for a chat. She had heard that there had been snowstorms in Scotland already and hoped that her daughter wasn't affected by them.

She then began to wonder what the weather was like in Kolkata. India was one country that Felicity had never visited, and try as she might, she couldn't picture John there at all. She missed him enormously and was already entertaining romantic fantasies about his return. But of course, she admonished herself, such dreams were utterly ridiculous at her age. Moreover it was clear that women weren't really his cup of chai. There was no point whatsoever in hoping that John's feelings for her were anything other than protective and platonic. But in spite of all this she couldn't help feeling aroused by this man. He was British certainly, and yet he carried an air of foreignness about him that spoke of intrigue and adventure. His dark eyes and raven black hair set her heart racing.

She threw her head back and ducked under a spout of bubbling water, as if to slough off these hopeless reveries. To fancy someone at her age after a long and happy marriage was futile. And yet… and yet. Perhaps she was finally rebelling against that insular world in which she had lived for most of her life: that Anglo-Saxon assumption of superiority that Alistair and his colleagues carried with them wherever they went. Anyway, she comforted herself, as she recalled a particularly intense and searching glance, it was better to be loved than feel alone, if only in her dreams.

*

"Oh hi, Peter, how are you?" Felicity said as her lift going up from the pool paused to admit him at level one. The steamy fug that hung around her was quickly dispelled as he entered through the double doors. She noticed that his jacket was spotted with rain.

"Hello, Felicity," he said tersely as he turned his back on her to press the button for level two. He remained in that position as the lift rose. The moment the doors opened again he had vanished along the corridor, even before she had time to gather her kit. This was beginning to feel a little odd.

By the end of the week, she had been snubbed by Peter yet again; Robert had looked the other way as he passed her in the corridor, and the older gentleman whom she had once confused for the Colonel nearly ran her over with his electric wheelchair, not even stopping to apologise. To cap it all, when she had called on Joan to enquire whether she had been feeling off colour, Joan had stuttered out that she was 'much too busy for a chat' and had instantly hung up. How she wanted to sink her face into Minou's soft fur and forget the world. Hadn't she always been convinced that pets made the best confidantes? Then she remembered that she had promised to feed Smokey, so maybe he would be able to offer her some sympathy instead. Of course, John would understand what was going on. He had told her to ring him if anything cropped up, but how could she? His time in India was far more important than her trivial concerns.

Tina
Lily's Launderette, Dunborough, England
November 25th 2017

"Hello, Tina. You doin' the washing on your own today love? Where's your little helper?"

"Afraid so, Albert. Alice has gone round to a friend's house for the day."

"That's nice for her. I thought you said her friend's father was a bit funny."

"She's got a new friend now. Nice family. They're as thick as thieves." Tina bent down to lift her washing and detergent tablets out of the laundry bag and place them in the machine. Sounds of rushing water soon filled the air and the clothes began to turn.

"You won't be goin' to the park then today I don't suppose. Why don't I make you a decent cup of tea instead while you wait?"

Tina accepted and willingly sat down while Albert busied himself behind his door.

"You know I do miss Lillian," Tina said as he handed her a mug. "You were so good to her Albert."

"I only did what any brother would do. We were close."

Tina sipped at her mug thoughtfully. She had befriended Lillian at school... such a funny little mite back then. Even as an adult she had seemed vulnerable.

"It was funny seeing Miss Jones here the other day, wasn't it?" Albert continued.

"Humph," she grumbled. "I thought it might have been her in her jeans and fancy jacket. Older women shouldn't dress like that in my mind, it's not proper."

Albert tried to protest.

"Mutton dressed up as lamb if you ask me," Tina insisted.

"She was all right Miss Jones... less stuck up than the rest of them. Did you know she used to use this launderette? Came to our house once around the time that our mum got ill. Really kind she was."

"Humph."

"They was good days at Sunnyvale."

"I know you thought so, Albert, but why couldn't we have gone to the school down the road like everyone else?"

"They looked after me and Lillian at that school they did, especially after our mum died. Mrs Harris was like a mother to us."

"Yeah. She was OK. I liked Mrs Harris."

"And they fed us well. Those school dinners... I've never forgotten them."

"You're right there," Tina enthused. "Remember that

183

treacle sponge and custard… it was evil."

They both laughed.

"You know I even liked Miss Jones at first," she conceded. "But in my mind Sunnyvale was a bad place. I saw what Mr Evans did to you and some of the other boys. It should never have been allowed."

"He was a nasty piece of work I'll give you that. And he said some pretty bad things to you too, Tina, don't think I didn't notice. But some of the other teachers were all right."

"You'll never guess what he's up to now. Gloria told me."

"What? Mr Evans? Surely he's dead by now."

"No… more's the pity. You must have heard of that man they call the Colonel? The landlord who gives everyone such a hard time? He was in the Dunborough Gazette recently, something about wrongful evictions."

Albert nodded. "I know the guy who works for him," he said. "Sometimes comes in here… youngish chap. Wouldn't trust him neither. Another nasty bit of work."

"Well, that's him… the landlord I mean."

"What? You don't mean old Mr Evans?"

"Better known nowadays as the Colonel."

Albert whistled with disbelief.

"Gloria did a spot of work in that posh block of flats down by the river. That's where he lives nowadays."

"No, I don't believe it. Mind you," he added, "they do say a leopard doesn't change his spots."

Tina lowered her voice as she noticed a young

student tucked up in the corner quietly reading a book. "Gloria doesn't want me to tell anybody about this, but he's really giving her a hard time. He's accusing her of being a thief."

"Your Gloria?" Albert expostulated. "That's ridiculous. Tina, if there's anything I can do to help, you just let me know."

"Thanks, Albert. You're one of the best. Do you still see Gary nowadays?"

"No, didn't you hear? He died a couple of years back… epileptic fit."

Shaking his head sadly, he gathered up their mugs and returned to his office, leaving Tina to become engrossed in the kaleidoscope of colours that swirled before her. Shocking pink and sugar candy for Alice; lime greens, oranges and mauves for Gloria; beige and bottle green for herself… trousers, shirts, dresses, tights and knickers… arms, legs, feet and torsos… all tangling and twisting together… like their lives, inextricably mixed. If anyone ever tried to separate them again, she would scream blue murder. Tina didn't sleep much at night nowadays and was beginning to feel drowsy.

Suddenly the main door opened and a man of around forty or fifty barged in, causing Tina's heart to give a lurch. As far as she could see he wasn't carrying any washing, and his clothes were very like those of a police officer or a security guard at the detention centre: navy trousers, blue shirt and a navy lamb's wool sweater topped with a dark blue nylon gilet. Even his black shoes looked highly polished and official. The man looked at her and nodded curtly. Tina's breaths came short and sharp, and a pain spread across her throat. She had to get out of there quickly.

Once in the street she took large gulps of cool air while holding on to a metal drainpipe to steady herself. Hadn't she half been expecting this? It was all very well their MP talking about biometric cards. You just had to look at what the Home Office had already done to her: they had been positively cruel and cold hearted. How could he be so sure that they wouldn't try and deport her now before her card came through? God only knows how she would cope if she ended up all on her own in Jamaica. Even Uncle James had long since died.

Painted bubbles danced and popped all over the window, obscuring her view, but a small space between them permitted Tina to peer inside. The man was talking to Albert now, most probably asking him about her. There was no way she would go back in, even though her wash had nearly finished, not while that man was there. So, Tina decided to take a walk in the park. The whole day ahead was hers alone. Albert would be sure to put her wash in the dryer for her and then put it somewhere safe. She would return to collect it after dark. And if they came looking for her at home, she had already decided what she would do. No one would ever dream of looking in Winston's fitted wardrobe.

The shops were busy that day, and family groups thronged the streets. But no matter how long Tina had lived around Dunborough, she always felt like an outsider. Everyone noticed her brown skin. Some people would look away quickly as if suddenly shocked, while others just stared rudely. She tried not to care. But she did. Soon she had left the shops behind, passed through the 'posh quarter' with the old fancy houses and big cars, and was entering the park through the heavy iron gates. At last she could breathe more easily. The overhanging shrubbery half concealed her as she strolled under the thinning canopy of autumn leaves. She loved this park whatever the weather, whatever the season. Her mum used to bring her here after a day on the wards, and she in turn had brought Gloria as a tiny tot. Now dearest Alice was her constant companion. Four generations of her family were attached to this soil. Four generations had watched the seasons turn, while newly planted saplings slowly and surely turned into giant trees. She'd be damned if anyone took this away from her.

Felicity
Avon Court, Dunborough, England
November 30th 2017

Felicity was getting used to solitude. If no one was willing to talk to her, she may as well be living in France. At least her French neighbours would be affable, not like the cold fish that surrounded her here. She had been counting the days until John's return, but he hadn't been in touch since he left so she couldn't be sure when that would be. Instead, she rang her children, and Gloria occasionally, just for a friendly chat. But she resisted the temptation to make a call to India. Food and drink, as always, proved to be a great comfort. It was late afternoon and she was now returning from a quick trip to the supermarket where she had bought some filleted duck and fresh vegetables to create a stir fry. She glanced into the display case on her way to the lift and smiled. Picasso never failed to impress.

As she approached the open doors, a strange man barged in front of her. She pressed the button for the first floor and turned to acknowledge him. It was clear that he didn't fit in here, for in spite of his smartish jacket and trousers, there was a food stain on his tie, and as for his garish trainers, they were completely wrong. He was carrying some kind of nylon holdall, and when the lift doors opened on their floor the man didn't move. Felicity turned back in order to speak to him.

"It doesn't go any further," she advised, before heading for her apartment. But when she turned again, the lift doors had closed and the man was nowhere to be seen.

The stir fry was delicious, even if she said it herself. She had found a new organic food shop which sold good vegetables, including bean sprouts which she loved, and the duck had been nice and tender. All she needed now was a decent espresso and life wouldn't seem quite so bad after all. As she placed her cup under the nozzle of the coffee machine, the lights suddenly went out. She stood stock still for a moment, wondering what to do. She had drawn the patio curtains earlier and the room was as dark as a tomb. There was a torch somewhere, she knew that, so Felicity began to grope through the kitchen drawers, trying hard not to panic. Finally, she found it.

"Damn, I forgot to replace the batteries," she cursed.

Slowly she edged towards the sofa which loomed like a ship in the fog. Feeling for the heavy curtains she drew them aside and the room immediately brightened. Now that she could see better, she poured herself an extra glass of wine and returned to the sofa, ready to sit it out until the electricity in the building was restored. The funny thing was, when she went out onto the patio to see if Smokey was there, she noticed that every single light in the rest of the building continued to blaze.

"Have you tried the mains switch?" Emily asked when she phoned her.

"Of course, I'm not that stupid. It's still up."

"Strange," Emily remarked.

The electricity returned less than an hour later, so Felicity watched the television late into the evening, trying to forget her concerns. But the next night, just before she was about to go to bed, it happened again.

"There must be an intermittent fault, Mum. I wouldn't worry," Emily soothed as Felicity cowered under the bedclothes and whispered into her mobile phone. "Have you made sure all the doors and windows are properly locked?"

After the call, Felicity continued to fret until suddenly the radio burst into life and her bedside light was restored. She reached to turn it off again and eventually fell asleep. The next morning she decided to go for a long walk. The town would be busy with Saturday shoppers so she headed for the canal towpath. A society had been formed to restore this stretch of waterway, but Felicity hoped that they wouldn't totally denude the banks. In spring they were lined with water irises and buttercups, and even as winter approached wildflowers persisted amongst the blades of grass. A water vole suddenly shot out from the bank creating a 'v' shaped wake as it headed for the other side. She smiled. It felt good to be in touch with nature again. Perhaps she should spend more time in her cottage in France. She'd give Madame le Brun a call and see if it was free in January, and maybe go down by train. The hellebores would be appearing in the woods by then, and she would seek out that little cache of violets that always arrives around Christmas Day. If it proved too cold for walking, she could always snuggle up by the log fire, something that she had missed in her new urban environment.

By the time Felicity returned home, she was feeling in much better spirits. Perhaps, she reflected, it had been foolish to expect to have a great rapport with her fellow Brits. Too much had changed over the decades. England was no longer the same country that had formed her. After a short work out in the gym followed by a swim, she returned to her apartment, planning to settle down and read before enjoying a late supper. Soon the haunting voice of Nina Simone filled the air as she searched for her Kindle.

"Alexa, please turn up the spots," she instructed. At that precise moment the music cut out and the lights died. "Oh no, not again," she groaned. Fortunately, this time she had not drawn the curtains, but in spite of the borrowed light from the town, she felt angry and frustrated.

"You mean you didn't report it to the electricity company?" Emily admonished, when she rang her daughter for comfort. "It's the weekend now. They'll not be able to send anybody out until Monday."

"I just thought…"

"Doesn't your Management Committee do anything about these things?"

"I did ring them after the first time, but they didn't take it too seriously. It is only intermittent after all."

Felicity agreed to get onto them again the next day, while Emily promised to be there if her mother needed to ring again. Felicity checked her Kindle. It was almost fully charged, so she snuggled up to read, draping a woollen rug over her knees to keep warm until all heating and lights could be restored. She read for well over an hour, so engrossed that she failed to notice that the room was still in darkness. Then her mobile phone rang. It was Gloria.

"Hi, Flic, how ya doin'?"

Felicity felt delighted. Gloria was sure to cheer her up. But when she told her about the power cuts her friend sounded suspicious.

"That doesn't sound right to me. Why don't I get my friend Joseph to come round tomorrow. He's a qualified electrician. If he can't tell you what's going on, nobody can."

"Thanks, Gloria. That would be great. I'll be in all day, so just give me a ring before you come."

"Actually, I rang to invite you to an exhibition of modern art. It's being held in the rooms above the shop next Saturday evening. I'm supposed to be serving drinks and things, but they said I could bring a guest. Would you like to come?"

"Oh, how kind of you to think of— aaarrgghh!" Felicity's sudden screech reverberated down the line. She could hear Gloria calling her name on the other end of the phone, but for a while she was unable to speak. Then she said hesitantly, "Gloria, I think somebody's just thrown a stone at the window."

"I'm coming round," Gloria announced. "Don't do anything. Make sure all your doors are locked. I'll be there in five."

By the time she arrived, Felicity had already plucked up the courage to venture outside, where she had found a small sharp rock lying on the patio. It was sitting now on the coffee table, and Gloria took it to the window to examine it more closely.

"Someone had to throw this with some force," she declared. "What's been going on, Flic? Is somebody trying to frighten you?"

They sat down together in the dim light while Felicity began to explain. She was going to have to tell Gloria that she was not only being ostracised, but that her friend was still being branded as a thief. Before she had finished, there was a sharp buzz as the electricity returned; the sudden brightness dazzled them. At that precise moment they both noticed a large crack that spread like an evil web across the top of the right hand patio door.

"Right," Gloria said. "There's no way you're staying

here on your own. I'll ring Mum and tell her I'll be back in the morning."

Gloria brought Joseph around early that Sunday evening. Felicity had offered to cook them some supper while Joseph tried to ascertain what the problem might be. After checking a few things with his special equipment, he declared that he was stumped.

"Never mind," Felicity said breezily. "It's Monday tomorrow, so I'll get onto the Management Committee again and give them what for. At least this has given me the chance to meet you, Joseph, and of course I'm always delighted to see Gloria."

She had made a tempura batter and was now standing at the stove ready to fry up some calamari rings and some shrimps, while Joseph and Gloria sat at the dining table drinking beer and wine. She had already placed some dipping sauces and candles in the centre of the table in readiness.

"Here we are," she announced, "tuck in."

Felicity sat at the head of the table and smiled broadly as she watched her guests delight in the meal that she had produced. It was almost worth being scared, to learn who your true friends were.

"Cheers," she called, raising her own glass to meet the others. With that, the lights went out.

"Joseph," Gloria called out in alarm.

But he was already barging his way towards the door. By the time he reached the corridor, he realised it was only Felicity's flat that had been plunged into darkness.

He raced to the lift, which was rising now, heading past their floor and up towards the roof. Ignoring that, he pushed open the fire door and descended the back staircase to the basement. To his right he could see the swimming pool and a door marked 'GYMNASIUM'. Somebody must have been swimming for he could hear splashing. The smaller corridor to his left was only dimly lit, but at the end he found exactly what he was looking for. Facing him was a heavy louvre iron door. It was, of course, firmly locked. At this point, as he told them later, he could do no more.

"There you are at last," Gloria said with relief as he reappeared. "If you leave the door open, we can get some extra light from the corridor."

Joseph was panting slightly. He took a gulp of sparkling water to recover.

"Should we eat?" she urged. "Flic's lovely cooking is getting cold."

Five tall red candles set in a large candelabra cast a warm glow over the proceedings. As they shared their seafood supper, Joseph worked out his plan.

"How long before the lights usually come on again?" he asked.

"Oh, I'm not sure. About an hour usually, maybe more."

"I have a pretty good idea what's going on. Don't be surprised if I rush off again when the lights return."

Felicity met Gloria's eyes.

"You will be careful, won't you," Gloria cautioned.

After supper they continued sitting around the table chatting in the half-light, drinking coffee that Felicity had made with her Belotti on the gas ring, and snacking on chocolate. Felicity had warmed to Joseph straight away. She liked men with strong opinions. Gloria talked about Tina, and the next stage in their struggle for justice from the Home Office. She also told Felicity more about her job. All of a sudden, their light was restored.

Joseph jumped up and raced to the end of the corridor. He burst through the fire door, leaping down the back staircase three steps at a time until he reached the basement. Barely able to catch his breath, he crouched with his back against the fire door and very slowly raised his phone towards the tiny window above his head. He heard the iron door at the end of the corridor close with a heavy clang. A lock was turned. Then footsteps, as someone approached the lift. Joseph leaned back hard against the door to prevent it being opened and activated his camera phone: once, twice, three times. Then he heard the lift doors open and released his breath. Stowing his phone into his pocket, he waited until the doors closed again and noted the time on his watch the moment it hummed into action. Standing now outside the lift doors he continued to time it until it reached its destination: ten… fifteen… twenty… twenty-five… thirty seconds. He heard the lift doors open and close some distance above him. Shortly afterwards he stepped into the lift himself and timed his own ascent to the first floor: five... ten... fifteen seconds. Then he was released.

They were sitting together on the sofa as Joseph related all this to Gloria and Felicity and prepared to share the photographs on his phone.

"I hope to God I captured him," he said. "The light wasn't great. But whoever is interfering with Flic's electricity supply is coming from the top floor and he's got access to the substation in the basement. There must be a circuit breaker for each flat in there."

He switched his phone on as the other two crowded around him. The first image drew a blank. The second showed a man's head and shoulders in profile. The third showed the back of his head.

"I've seen him before," Felicity exclaimed. "It's the bloke in the lift. I saw him the first day it happened."

"What's he got to do with the geezer on the top floor?" Joseph wondered. "He's ancient, isn't he?"

Gloria grabbed the phone and was studying the second image more closely. "I'll tell you who it is," she said with certainty. "It's the Colonel's sidekick. You see him around town. Everyone says he's a nasty bit of work."

There was a sudden loud rap on the open door and Gloria screamed.

"Can I come in? I hope it's not too late."

Gloria and Joseph looked at each other in surprise.

"John! Of course, come in!" Felicity's face beamed all the messages that she had hoped to conceal.

"Hi everyone," he said, quickly taking in the situation. "You must be Gloria," John said as he proffered his hand. "It's good to meet you properly at last. I'm glad to see Flic's got some company. And you must be…?"

"Joseph. Pleased to meet you, John."

They shook hands firmly.

"Look, Flic, I'm sorry I didn't warn you. I wasn't going to get in touch with you until the morning, but then I heard voices and saw that your door was open. Is this OK? It's really great to see you again." He sat himself down in an adjacent armchair and began to complain about his flight, chatting merrily away. But soon he realised that all was not well. After listening to Gloria's explanation, John said grimly, "Gloria. I really must thank you for looking after Flic like this. It is utterly atrocious the way this man has treated you, and now he's victimising her too. I'll stay here tonight to make sure that Flic's OK. And tomorrow I'm going to the police. I assume you could identify this man, Joseph?"

"We've got him on camera," Joseph, Felicity and Gloria told him in gleeful unison.

"You could collect evidence of the outages too," Joseph added. "There's not a lot a smart meter can't show you."

"Brilliant. With your evidence, Joseph, and everything else that's been going on, I think we've caught our man fair and square this time. Harassment is

198

a serious crime. I can't thank you two enough."

Joseph and Gloria grinned at each other. Felicity was beginning to feel like a spare part in a detective novel. But as she looked from one to the other, she felt sublimely happy. For now it was abundantly clear that these friends were of the very best variety, and she no longer felt alone. But one problem remained. Where on earth was John going to sleep?

Felicity
Wood Parade, Dunborough, England
December 12th 2017

The police decided not to prosecute George Evans, but gave him a very strong warning never to indulge in harassment again. When he resigned from his position on the Residents' Committee, citing failing health, the others asked Felicity to join them, just as John had suggested they would. She thanked them, but politely refused their offer. Fortunately, the final apartment in the development had since become occupied by a retired couple from Wales, so Joan did get her wish to co-opt some female support. By then, John and Felicity had become regular walking companions. They would often discuss how George Evans had almost succeeded in his attempt to cast the blame on Gloria.

"I think he's got secret security cameras that enable him to see when the coast is clear. Then he can sneak down and carry out his evil ways," John suggested.

Felicity had grasped the theme with alacrity. "And I think he's got control over those lifts. No one else knows how to operate them beyond the first floor, apart from him and his henchman. I reckon he can nip down to the foyer and back up again like a 'deus ex machina'."

"You know, I'm generally not too keen on conspiracy theories, but on this occasion, Detective Inspector Jones, I think you might well be right."

They mostly strolled along the riverbanks, where Felicity liked to chat with fellow walkers and the occasional fly fisherman. But one December afternoon, John suggested that they take a walk in town instead. They were both fascinated by Dunborough's magnificent architecture and felt that they still had a lot to explore. Felicity also derived an illicit pleasure from visiting those elegant Georgian terraces, covertly peeping inside people's windows to see what kind of furnishings they had chosen. It was all pretty standard opulent stuff: heavy William Morris style curtains, dark velvet upholstery and period furniture. However, one home in her old terrace happily flaunted this code. She had seen it advertised in the local estate agents and had whooped in delight at the vast stripped down rooms; bizarre light fittings; walls and carpets in deep purples and reds, and abstract paintings greater in area than Gloria's friend's tiny kitchen. She had made a special visit to ogle this daring property, but it had been a fruitless trip. From the outside, one would never have guessed that it was different from the rest. She nursed a hope that somewhere, on some top floor, a budding artist lived and worked in his tiny garret; in reality, every last square inch, from the basement to the eaves, was now monopolised by the wealthy. Living there as an impecunious teacher would have been out of the question nowadays. She made this observation to John and they both agreed that their 'baby boomer' generation had been lucky to enjoy so many more opportunities.

"It's tough on the young nowadays," she reflected, "having to struggle while they see others with money to burn." They were walking past a row of parked cars, each displaying a resident's badge to ward off fines. "What use is a Porsche like that for example? Just imagine travelling any distance at all, cooped up in there. Where would you even stow your luggage?"

"All they have to say is 'our other car is a Bentley'," John quipped, "and this time it is almost certainly true."

"Where on earth do these people get all their money from? It's beyond obscene."

"*Plus ça change*," John grumbled. "These houses were built for the rich, and now only the rich can afford to live here again. Of course, you do realise that many of the historic homes around here were built with money derived from slave trading."

"I do, unfortunately."

"You know, Flic, the inequality in our country disgusts me."

She was growing ever more deeply in love with John, and thoroughly enjoyed his righteous anger. It had been so different living with Alistair whose life had become dominated by business meetings and company takeovers. Not that she had any reason to grumble. She had loved her husband, but their wealth had begun to set them apart and made her feel slightly uncomfortable. When she had tried to explain this to him, he hadn't really understood and had mocked her for being a 'puritanical Northerner'.

That afternoon Felicity suggested that they prolong their walk and head up the hill towards Wood Parade. This crescent had been designed by the same architect and in a similar style to the one she had lived in. It also had the added virtue of a commanding view over the town.

"The last time I came up here," Felicity panted, "was in my little Fiat. I had been asked to deliver some parcels to elderly residents after our school harvest festival."

They had reached the top of the hill now and turned to survey the view. Dunborough lay below them to the south-west, nestled in a perfect pudding bowl, while the setting wintery sun cast oblique rays over its mellow stone buildings.

"If I remember rightly, the air used to be thick with smoke back then. You would see great puffs of blue black smoke billowing from the chimneys and hanging about above the town. Do you remember that, John?"

"We're a part of history," John reflected, but Felicity didn't much like that observation. "No little Fiats to be seen around here nowadays," John observed, nodding at all the large cars that were parked head to tail around the curve. "You wouldn't even have been allowed to park here."

Felicity had increased her pace and was heading towards the end of the row. She liked to observe how each entrance was graced by a flight of stone steps leading up to a pair of elegant white stone pillars. Suddenly she had become lady of the household descending towards a carriage, while its horses fretted and fussed impatiently on the cobbles.

"I couldn't have borne those tight waists and cumbersome dresses," she announced out loud.

"Oh, I think you would have looked extremely elegant," John assured her, "but that's not to say you don't look good in those trainers. That's a great hat by the way."

"Thank you kindly, sir." Felicity gave a slight curtsey.

"Is this the house you're looking for?"

They had come to the end of the row.

"Yes, I'm pretty sure that's where she lived." Felicity was holding on to the top of the railings now as she leaned over to peer down into the basement below. "You know, I've never forgotten that experience. There was me balancing this wooden box full of leeks and potatoes, apples, onions and stuff like that, not to mention a big fat marrow. It was a struggle getting down those steps without dropping anything, I can tell you. When I got to the door, I knocked hard on that iron knocker. Can you see it? It's amazing to think that it's still there after all those years. Anyway, no one answered. I knocked twice, maybe three times, but still no one came to the door. I was getting impatient because I had a couple more boxes to deliver and wanted to get home for my tea. In the end I realised why I had to wait so long. When the door opened, I saw the oldest, most crippled lady I had ever seen in my life. It would seem that she was living there alone, utterly independent and proud to boot. She was bent double, but you know she still reached up to take the box from me and refused to let me carry it inside for her. She didn't say a word. It was hard to gauge whether she was grateful or not. But I'll tell you this… I felt so so guilty for dragging her to that door."

"I'm sure she was… grateful I mean."

"I don't want to grow old like that. I'd like to think that I could maintain my independence but…"

"I've treated a lot of very old people in my time. In Malawi the elders would always be surrounded by their extended families. But you don't see that very often in London. And don't imagine Dunborough is any different. I've done quite a few locums here. You come across an awful lot of loneliness and neglect. I don't know what the answer to it all is. Certainly not more privately run care homes, of that I'm certain."

"All I know is that I have never forgotten her. I think it was the contrast between us that shocked me most. We were both living in similar basement flats, and I suppose in a way we were both lonely. Yet my adult life was just beginning, and hers was nearing its end. And now…" Felicity unfurled her hands from the railings and turned away. "What's wrong with our society, that so many people are left on the outside?"

John paused. "Flic," he said hesitantly, "if I were to make a suggestion, would you consider it seriously before giving me an answer. I've been thinking about this for a while."

She felt a flutter in the pit of her stomach. Surely… he couldn't be…? If she hadn't known him better, she might have thought that he was about to propose marriage. But that was preposterous. She had been telling herself that for weeks.

And yet, that is exactly what followed. They were walking slowly now back towards the town.

"You know I've always loved you from a distance," he professed. "I hope you don't think I've been too slow in telling you."

"Only about half a century," she mocked.

John failed to smile. "But what is it they say… it's never too late? Why don't we share our remaining years together? Just you and me. Please don't say no straight away, Flic. Please give it some thought."

"But what about…?"

"Bill?"

Felicity nodded.

"We discussed this before he died. He was adamant that I shouldn't spend the rest of my days in mourning. He positively wanted me to find another soulmate."

"But…?"

"And as for being gay, I firmly believe that it's the relationship that is key, not the gender."

"John… I…"

"Not now, Flic. Just please give it some thought."

"I will," Felicity whispered. "I promise."

Her companion suddenly brightened. "Anyway, is that why Miss Jones brought me up here? To talk about old age? Come on, I fancy a drink. I know a nice pub in town. If we're lucky we'll be in time to get a seat by the fire before the evening rush."

*

By the time they got to the Minstrel it was already dark and they were frozen through. Unfortunately, the biggest table close to the fire had been reserved for a large party, and the smaller one was occupied by a couple of men who looked as if they were having a few pints after work.

"Let's slip in here," John suggested, pointing to one of the four tall wooden booths close by.

Felicity had always imagined them to be excellent venues for secret assignations. It all felt exceedingly romantic.

"What are you having?"

"No, you sit there. It's my turn. You bought the drinks last time."

"I do like an emancipated lady," John teased.

As Felicity was struggling to carry their drinks back to the booth, she noticed Gloria coming through the door. She was about to put their drinks down on the table and go over to greet her when she stopped herself. A number of other people were coming in behind, stamping their feet and rubbing their hands as they escaped from the cold. Everyone was laughing and happy. Felicity noticed how nearly all of her fellow drinkers had suddenly stopped talking and turned around to watch the proceedings.

"Here's our table," Gloria announced. "Please sit down everyone. Mum, you go first and sit at the head, as our guest of honour. Alice, you can sit next to her if you like. Winston and Angela, you'll probably want to sit together over there. Mr Smith, how about you sit at the other end, and Joseph and I will sit here. How's that everyone?"

By this time Felicity had slipped into the booth alongside John.

"I assume that's the famous Tina."

"Hush! I feel a bit like a spy."

"Right, everybody, what are you having to drink?"

Gloria seemed to be in a buoyant mood, and Felicity realised just how much she missed her about the place. She assumed that Joseph was now Gloria's regular man and hoped so much that it was going well. Angela was the only white person in the group and seemed to be attached to Winston. Meanwhile, Gloria was standing up again and heading for the bar, accompanied by Mr

208

Smith, an older man, who was offering to help.

"Drink up," John urged. "I was thinking, if you're willing, I could offer you a bite of supper at my place."

Felicity failed to answer.

"Flic? What do you say to supper together?"

"You know I've wanted to meet Tina again ever since I realised who she was," she whispered. "It's such an amazing coincidence that her daughter has been helping me."

"She was a pupil of yours?"

"A very special and unusual pupil, but no one realised."

"Then why not just go over and say hello?"

"She doesn't want to meet me. She believes I let her down. Apparently, I'm 'a stuck-up bitch', which, if you come to think of it, is probably true."

"Then just leave her. We all have our grievances from the past, and they're not always rational. Just let it go."

"I can't. It haunts me, it really does. You know, I must have hurt her so badly, without realising. I tore her off a strip one day because she and her friend were playing me up. Then she got angry and accused me of targeting her just because she was black."

John groaned.

"Maybe I did. Maybe I was unwittingly racist. How can I possibly be sure that I wasn't? We're all slightly racist somewhere deep inside, in spite of our best intentions."

"That's way in the past. Anyway, if you're a racist, then I'm Donald Trump."

Felicity laughed and gulped the rest of her wine.

"After that happened, she wrote me the most amazing poem, every bit as good as one of those sixties protest songs. Looking back on it now, I realise it was a plea for help."

"I don't suppose you kept it?"

"I so wish that I had. Do you want to know what I did about it? Not a thing... nada... niente... rien du tout. I never even told her how good it was."

John shook his head ruefully.

"Besides, I couldn't stand working there much longer. George Evans was making snide comments about the place and the atmosphere was absolutely toxic. So I handed in my resignation and abandoned her, along with all those other poor kids, half of whom would have been better off in their own local schools."

They both remained silent. Then Felicity suddenly brightened.

"How about that supper you promised? If the offer still stands, I'd love to take you up on it. Mind you, I expect haute cuisine, nothing less."

"Mais oui, bien sûr."

"I'll just say goodbye to Gloria and Alice on the way out and catch you up on the street." But Felicity stayed put because at that moment Gloria was standing up and calling on her friends to raise their glasses to Tina.

"Here's to a brilliant mum and grandmother," she

called.

"Hear, hear," agreed Mr Smith raising his pint.

"Yes, Nana, cheers," Winston agreed. "Don't let them ever do that to you again."

Felicity didn't like to move now, continuing to observe everyone agreeing with Gloria and knocking back their various drinks. Then Gloria spoke again.

"Mum, we just want to say how relieved and pleased we are that the government have finally given in. You do have the absolute right to remain here."

"We never doubted it."

"Here's to that biometric card."

"Hear, hear."

"Too bloody right. It was a disgrace what they did to you, Tina. You're as British as they come."

"British?" a jeering voice broke the mood.

The whole pub fell silent as everyone's attention turned towards the slightly drunken man sitting at the adjacent table.

"British my arse," he continued. "You should go back to where you came from and take the rest of your bleedin' friends with you."

With that he pulled himself out of his captain's chair and lurched towards the bar carrying two empty beer glasses. His friend seemed to have shrunk beneath the collar of his denim jacket. Meanwhile, the buzz of pub conversation quickly picked up again as if nothing had happened.

Felicity and John had frozen in their seats and were

wondering how to play things when the man returned with two more beers, weaving a slightly indirect route towards his table.

"Here y'are, Jim," he said affably as he placed the beer glasses down. Then before sitting down himself, he leaned over the neighbouring table to address Angela. "And I don't know what you're doin', love, hanging out with that monkey there. Pretty girl like you should do better for herself."

Felicity turned anxiously towards the bar. The landlord was an honest man; surely, he should be trying to turf this nasty brute out. However, he seemed totally ignorant of the current happenings, polishing glasses furiously with his tea towel. It was then that Joseph made his presence felt, ready to square up to this bullying white man. Standing face to face, he addressed him in a cold controlled voice.

"Look, mate. Don't you dare tell us that we don't belong here. Me and my British friends have got as much right to be here as anybody else. So just get out of my face will you."

The other man, who was definitely worse for wear, hesitated. The whole pub had fallen quiet once more as everyone waited to see what would happen next. But before the bully could summon up further insults, Joseph pre-empted him. He spun around as if he were addressing every single one of his fellow drinkers.

"Just remember, mate," he proclaimed in his deep and tuneful voice. "We are here, because YOU. WERE.

THERE."

Felicity took a silent intake of breath. Boy, did she admire Gloria's choice of men!

"Very well said, sir," John muttered.

It had become clear to Felicity that John was struggling to stand by any longer and watch this assault on Gloria's party. Ignoring Felicity, he now pushed himself up from the bench, brushed past the two white men and approached Gloria's table with his hand extended in greeting.

"Hi, Gloria," he said at the top of his voice. "It's great to see you again."

Felicity soon caught up with him and stood by his side.

"Would you very much mind if we joined in your celebration. I know Flic here has been so anxious for Tina and would love to meet her."

Felicity gasped with embarrassment. She hardly dared look anyone in the face. But there was no stopping John, for now he had turned towards the smaller table, where the bully had slumped into his seat.

"Ah, Mr Burton. You seem to be disturbing these friends of ours. Don't you think it would be a good idea if you were to leave? By the way, how is your mum faring now that she's gone into that home?"

Felicity was enjoying the look on this man's face immensely.

"Er... er... she's all right, Dr Cherry... thanks very much for asking... she's doing OK, thank you..." He paused, as if struggling to know what to do next. His shoulders had slumped as his belligerence shrivelled inside him. "Look, Dr Cherry, I didn't mean no harm. Me and my mate was just havin' a bit of fun like…" Within seconds both men had fled the pub, leaving two full pints of beer sitting on their table.

When Felicity finally looked up, she saw Gloria grinning at her.

"Thanks," was all she said.

Then Felicity dared to snatch a look at Tina and her hopes sank. There was that defiant teenager looking back at her, as hostile and prickly as ever.

Alice
Wood Terrace, Dunborough, England
March 22nd 2022

"Are they the king and queen now?" Alice asked her mother. She wasn't really so stupid as to believe it, but that's how it seemed as images of the Duke and Duchess of Cambridge's tour of the Caribbean appeared on the late night television news.

"They're certainly behaving as if they are," said Joseph in disgust. "Parading around in all those fancy clothes. OK, so I've not got a lot of time for the Queen either, but if anyone's going to visit Jamaica, I'd rather it was her."

"Do you like her dress, Mum?"

"It's a bit fancy in my mind, all that lace and stuff."

"She does look very pretty though."

"What's that she's got on her head? It looks more like a bloomin' plate than a hat," Joseph protested, thrusting himself forward and continuing to yell at the screen. "Don't you lot get it? You're not welcome in Jamaica anymore."

215

Alice sighed. It was nice having Joseph there, but he did get a bit worked up over politics and things. Gloria and Alice were sitting alongside him on the sofa. They were a family now, ever since Tina had gone back to her old job and her flat in the big city. She hadn't seen very much of her nana recently because of Covid. But she was coming to visit them at the weekend and Alice couldn't wait to see her.

"Why're they visiting Jamaica? Nana says that she never wants to set foot there ever again."

"Well, that's because you and me and Winston are living here, and she doesn't want to leave us. We're all of us British now."

"But what's wrong with Jamaica?"

Joseph decided to intervene. "Jamaica is a beautiful country, Alice. You gotta be proud of it."

"Maybe we can all go there for a holiday together one day," suggested her mum.

Alice wasn't too sure. She had lots of plans but visiting Jamaica wasn't yet on her list. Come September she would be learning Spanish, and she wanted to visit Spain more than anywhere else in the whole world. Although, of course, she'd give the bull fighting a miss. That was just brutal.

"Mum could come with us," Gloria continued, "and show us where she was born."

"Joseph, do you know that my nana came here on an aeroplane all by herself, when she was only ten?" Alice pulled an amazed face. "I'm nearly eleven, and I don't

216

think I could ever be that brave."

The news had moved on to a scene in which Prince William and his wife were being driven through the crowds in an old-fashioned Land Rover. He was standing to attention, dressed in fancy white military attire with a large blue sash draped across his chest. This angered Joseph so much that he stormed off to the kitchen. Gloria and Alice continued to watch as more images of the visiting Royals appeared on their screen. Catherine in a long flowing yellow dress, descending aircraft steps; Catherine in an emerald-green ball gown being greeted by the governor general of Jamaica and his wife; Catherine in a multi-coloured cotton dress playing a drum and surrounded by local Rastafarian musicians in Kingston.

"That's where Bob Marley lived," Gloria explained.

When Joseph had moved in, he had brought some Bob Marley CDs with him and Alice had thought his music was really cool. Catherine was now being shown in a powder-blue knee-length number receiving a bouquet from a small Barbadian girl.

"Looks more like a fashion parade than a royal tour of the Caribbean," her mother grumbled. "Don't tell me she packed all those dresses herself."

"Oh, Mum," Alice complained. "At least she tries to look nice."

Alice liked Catherine, and sometimes wondered whether she would like to be a royal princess herself, just like Meghan Markle. But then, she had decided, there wouldn't be time for all the other important things in life that she planned to do.

"Oh no, I don't believe it." Joseph had returned to the sofa with a glass of beer in his hand. He was watching as the royal couple, dressed more casually now, bent down to bestow touches on the outstretched hands of little children as they clamoured and cheered from behind a wire fence. "This is more than I can bear. Who do they think they are, White Saviours or something?"

But the news broadcast was taking on a different tone from the usual reportage of a royal visit. It had moved to a group of demonstrators who were carrying the green, yellow and black flag of Jamaica.

"Do you know what that flag means Alice?"

Alice shook her head, trying not to look too uninterested.

"It says 'hardships there are, but the land is green and shineth'," he explained.

But Alice was becoming more curious now as lots of angry protesters filled the screen carrying placards which demanded 'Sey Yuh Sorry' and 'Apologise'. Two young Jamaican women held aloft a large cloth banner between them. She gasped with horror at the image that they carried: a large pair of black hands bound together at the wrists by long metal chains. Written in large black letters along the bottom of the banner was the word 'Reparation'. This was something that she really did need Joseph to explain.

"Joseph, what does that mean?"

"It's time for bed now, honey," Gloria said. "You've got school tomorrow. If you go upstairs and get your jammies on, I'll come up in a minute."

"But what does reparation mean? And why were black people in chains? Joseph, will you tell me what it means? After all, I'm Jamaican too, and I really have to know."

Alice
Grove Park, Dunborough, England
March 23rd 2022

The next day, Alice made her own way to John and Felicity's new flat after school. Every Wednesday she and Felicity would go for a swim in the pool, often accompanied by Joan, who had become infinitely more pleasant to be around. John said it was all due to the Colonel's departure, but Felicity disagreed, saying that Alice had simply charmed Joan, just like she had charmed everyone else. Afterwards, Alice would always stay for tea. John had shown her how to cook dahl, and today he had promised they could make pooris together. The sun felt unusually warm on her neck. She spotted some daffodils and celandines growing alongside the path that led from the weir and crouched down to pick a small posy as a gift for Felicity. The whole world seemed to be waking up but, in spite of this, Alice didn't feel quite so bright and cheerful inside.

"What's up, doc?" John asked her as he opened the door.

She liked John. He always seemed to understand her moods. Alice flopped down on the sofa, throwing her rucksack on the floor beside her feet.

"Buttercups, eh?" he said, indicating towards the posy in her hand.

"Celandines actually."

Felicity had just come down from the roof garden, where she had been looking out for Alice's arrival, and Alice noticed John and Felicity exchange glances. Adults could be so annoying sometimes.

"You know, I could really do with catching that last bit of sunshine out there," Felicity mused. "What would you say to a walk to the park instead of swimming, while John cooks tea?"

"But what about Joan? Won't she miss us? And what about the pooris? John promised…"

"They have to be cooked at the very last minute so they stay puffed up," he explained. "I've already made the dough, but you can help me fry them after you get back."

Alice brightened slightly.

"As long as you get back before six you can help me make the onion bhajis too. How does that sound?"

Ten minutes later Felicity kissed John goodbye and closed the door on their new flat. George Evans had been happy to sell it to them and, with his departure, daffodils, crocuses and miniature roses bloomed in place of weeds on the roof garden terrace, and an olive tree thrived in its terracotta pot. As for the pervading smell of rotting fruit, that had been well and truly expunged. The lift from the top floor was working properly now, so she and Alice were soon stepping out into the vestibule. Alice lingered to look at the pretty bowl with its fighting matador and fierce bull, just like she always did, and trailed her finger over the glass. One day, she vowed, she would get to hold it between her hands. Although, of course, she was never ever ever going to approve of bull fighting, whatever anybody said.

"Park or river?" Felicity asked as they left the building.

"You promised you'd look into tennis lessons for me the next time we went to the park," Alice grumbled. She dreamed of becoming a tennis star like the Williams sisters. When she told other people they just laughed. But Alice was determined. She knew for certain that she was going to become the first British Women's Wimbledon champion since Virginia Wade.

Felicity hadn't laughed when Alice had mentioned it to her. "Go for it, Alice," she had exclaimed at the time. "You're a great swimmer, so why shouldn't you be good at tennis too? Why don't we ask your mum if we can enrol you for tennis lessons at the municipal courts?"

There was something about Felicity. She always made you feel good. Alice could never understand why her nana didn't much like Felicity, she really was so kind. Of course, her real nana would always come first, but sometimes it felt as though Felicity and John were her other nana and grandpa. But today, even though the sun was still shining, and they had decided to return via the tennis courts to check things out, Alice was still feeling a bit grumpy.

"How was school?" Felicity ventured.

"OK."

"Just OK?"

"Mmm. Not bad come to think of it."

"Do anything interesting?"

"I suppose so," Alice conceded. "But I didn't learn much from my teacher. I taught him something in fact."

"Good for you," Felicity laughed. "How about you teach me too?"

"I bet you don't know what reparation means, Flic."

"Mmm. Maybe not exactly…"

"Everybody had to share a new word with the rest of the class, so I taught them about reparation. Do you know that my great, great, great, great, great…" Alice grasped a breath. "… great, great grandmother was probably a slave in Jamaica?"

Felicity nodded. "You know, Alice, I saw the sugar plantations there once. They seemed to go on and on forever. I imagine it must have been very hard work."

"Do you realise how cruel the English people were to their slaves? They had to work every day in the hot sun, and they could never ever be free. You know, it just makes me feel very very sad."

223

"It makes me angry too, Alice, to think of all that suffering."

"Joseph said that English traders took people away from their homes in Africa to sell as slaves in Jamaica. Isn't that horrible? Mum believes our family probably came from the Yoruba tribe in West Africa, or maybe the Igbo. When I told my teacher, he said we could all do a topic about it."

"So what does your new word mean exactly?"

"Reparation? Joseph says reparation means making up for the bad things that you've done to somebody else. He says they should pay Jamaica a lot of money. What do you think?"

Felicity sighed. "That's a big question. Perhaps you should talk to John. I know he feels very strongly about it, just like Joseph does."

Alice felt puzzled, for what had John got to do with Jamaica? Maybe his skin was a bit brownish, but he certainly wasn't black. So, she asked Felicity about that too.

"You didn't know that John's mum was born in India?"

Alice shook her head.

"That was a British colony as well, and some people say that we should pay them reparation."

"Were there slaves in India?"

"No, Alice, but John says our country did some pretty terrible things out there, and that we should pay for it."

"Why does everyone want to live in this country

when it has done so many bad things?"

Felicity sighed long and hard but failed to answer. They had arrived at the park now, and she sat down on her favourite bench. Alice didn't feel like going on the swings that day, so she sat alongside her. An elderly couple walked past trailing a Jack Russell. They were clearly curious and couldn't help gawping as they went by. Alice wouldn't dream of pulling a face at them in front of Felicity, but she did know how cross it made her when people stared at them together like that. Felicity said that far too many people were stupid, and never looked beyond the colour of your skin. But then Joseph had told Alice that 'black is beautiful', so who was she to believe? Alice had decided that they were both right in their way.

Felicity remained silent, while Alice swung her legs to and fro under the bench, watching the poor little Jack Russell being yanked away from interesting smells by its impatient owners. The wind had dropped, and the whole park had fallen silent, as if it was holding its breath. Finally, Felicity answered her question.

"Alice darling, you've just asked me the one question that I can't answer."

But Alice knew that Felicity would answer it, just like she always did.

"You know, I often wonder why I live here too."

She had never seen Felicity look so serious before. It was almost as if she was going to cry.

"This country *has* done lots of very bad things," she

continued. "But I am British and so is John, and so are you and Winston, and your mum and your nana. So we all have to live here and care for one another. We have to be proud, and love what is good about our country, and fight what is bad."

Alice understood perfectly. In fact, Joseph felt the same way. He told her that she should fight bad things too.

"Do you think I should be an MP like Dawn Butler when I grow up, instead of becoming a tennis player?"

"What's wrong with both? You've got lots of time." She put her arm around Alice and drew her close.

"You know, Flic, I'm going to write a poem about my great great great… oh… whatever," Alice giggled. "But I'm going to write a poem about her working in the hot sun all the time, and never being free."

"Just like your nana. She wrote poetry too when she was a girl. Did you know that?"

Alice shook her head.

"You could ask her to help you."

"Were you really her teacher?"

"Yes, Alice, I was. But teachers don't always get things right you know. I wish I'd told your nana what a good poet she was. Will you tell her that from me, instead?"

Alice looked at her seriously and nodded.

"Promise?" Felicity insisted.

"Promise," Alice vowed.

Then she jumped down, ready to head for the big

swings. She suddenly felt happy again and was hoping that her best friend Jane might be there. But the swings lay empty. The breeze had returned and they were swaying backwards and forwards on their long chains, as if occupied by invisible children. Alice jumped up onto the middle swing and began to rock herself, gently at first, backwards and forwards, backwards and forwards. Then, as the arc of her motion grew, she threw back her head each time, and gazed at the sky while pointing her toes towards the budding trees.

"Careful you don't fall," she heard Felicity calling out anxiously from the bushes, as the iron chain gave a sudden jerk.

But Alice just laughed and pushed herself to go even higher. For didn't Felicity already know? This English Jamaican girl was heading for the stars.

Postscript
A note from the author, Joan Lewis
March 2022

On the 23rd of March 2022, Prince William addressed Jamaica's Prime Minister and other dignitaries.

"I strongly agree with my father, the Prince of Wales, who said in Barbados last year that the appalling atrocity of slavery forever stains our history. I want to express my profound sorrow. Slavery was abhorrent and it should never have happened. While the pain runs deep, Jamaica continues to forge its future with determination, courage and fortitude. The strength and shared purpose and courage of the Jamaican people, represented in your flag and motto, celebrates an invincible spirit."

He also expressed gratitude to the Windrush generation.

"We are forever grateful for the immense contribution that this generation and their descendants have made to British life, which continues to enrich and improve our society," he said.

To date, the wealth derived from the slave trade still

circulates within European society. No financial reparation has ever been paid. The compensation scheme for the cruel indignities and suffering that Windrush victims were illegally forced to bear remains largely undistributed. Some Windrush victims have since died.

BV - #0473 - 200423 - C0 - 197/132/13 - PB - 9781803781129 - Matt Lamination